KITTEN IN THE COLD

Mandy peered up the snowy slope to the ridge. Amber sat and shivered against the chimney. "Here, Amber!" Mandy edged up another rung. The kitten backed away.

Mandy leaned against the gutter and reached out with both hands. Her legs had begun to tremble. The icy wind whipped up loose snow and blew it in her face. "Amber, don't be scared. Come this way!"

In her confusion, Amber thought that Mandy's outstretched arms meant danger. She edged back again, almost lost her footing on the snow-covered ridge, and half slipped from sight. Mandy gasped. With a struggle, the kitten found her balance and cowered against the chimney.

"Any good?" Dr. Emily called.

"No!" Mandy looked desperately along the treacherous surface. "I'm coming down!"

Give someone you love a home!
Read about the animals of Animal Ark™

Kitten
in the Cold

Ben M. Baglio

Illustrations by Shelagh McNicholas

Cover illustration by
Mary Ann Lasher

AN
APPLE
PAPERBACK

SCHOLASTIC INC.
New York Toronto London Auckland Sydney
Mexico City New Delhi Hong Kong

Special thanks to Jenny Oldfield.
Thanks also to C. J. Hall, B.Vet.Med., M.R.C.V.S., for reviewing
the veterinary information contained in this book.

ISBN 0-439-09698-7

Text copyright © 1996 by Working Partners Ltd.
Original series created by Ben M. Baglio.
Illustrations copyright © 1996 by Shelagh McNicholas.

12 11 10 9 8 7 6 5 4   0 1 2 3 4/0

Printed in the U.S.A.   40
First Scholastic printing, November 1999

To the real Amber

TM

One

"Mandy, are you sure you know what you're doing?" Grandpa Hope asked as she lifted Smoky onto the kitchen table at Lilac Cottage.

Grandma tut-tutted. "For goodness sake, Tom, you can see that the cat is in good hands. Stop fretting and let Mandy get on with it." She bustled to fetch a small bottle of cleanser, a bowl of hot water, and some cotton balls.

"We'll need a towel," Mandy warned. "Smoky won't like having his ears cleaned. He'll try to shake his head. The cleanser gets everywhere."

Grandpa brought a striped red towel and spread it on the table. "That stuff's not too hot, is it?"

1

Mandy dipped the bottle into the hot water, while Smoky strolled up and down to investigate.

"Tom!" Grandma said. "Why don't you go into the living room and read a nice gardening magazine until we're finished in here? I don't know about Mandy, but you're making me nervous!"

Mandy grinned. "It's OK. It doesn't bother me." Her grandpa worried about two things in life, his garden and his cat. It was Grandpa who'd noticed something was wrong with Smoky's ear in the first place. He told Mandy that Smoky was always scratching it and shaking his head. Mandy had gone back to Animal Ark and asked her mom and dad what it could be.

"Ear mites," Adam Hope had suggested. "The bites could be infected." He'd stopped by the cottage to take a look and left Mandy there to treat poor Smoky's condition.

"Don't look!" Grandma told Grandpa, as Mandy settled Smoky and gently took hold of the scruff of his neck. "Do you need any help, Mandy?"

She shook her head. "Smoky's a good boy, aren't you? You're not going to struggle." Speaking soothingly, Mandy very carefully put a drop or two of lukewarm liquid into the cat's ear. "See, it's not too horrible, is it?"

Smoky opened his mouth wide and meowed.

"There." She massaged a spot just below his ear.

"What's that for?" Grandpa ventured forward for a closer look.

"To soften the earwax. I have to clear it out before I put some other drops in." She worked patiently, glad that Smoky didn't fidget. Taking a cotton ball, she wiped cleanser from the ear canal.

"Oops!" Grandpa stepped back, as suddenly Smoky shook his head. Drops splashed onto the towel.

"Almost done," Mandy promised. She finished off with a cotton swab, easing it down the ear to clean out the tiny, delicate folds of skin. Then Grandma handed her the bottle of medicine that Adam Hope had given them. Mandy held the dropper to the infected ear and let three or four drops fall. A quick final massage and the job was done.

"Will that do the trick?" Grandpa asked.

Mandy handed Smoky over to him. "Yes. The drops will kill the mites and cure the infection." She'd seen it done many times at the clinic, but this was the first time she'd been trusted to do it herself. She felt pleased that it had gone well.

"Excellent!" Grandpa beamed at her. "We'll make a vet of you yet."

"I hope so," Mandy sighed. She longed to follow in her mom and dad's footsteps and run the clinic with them.

"Long hours, lots of stress," Grandma reminded her. She cleared the table and put on a clean cloth. "It's not an easy job."

But Mandy couldn't think of anything she'd rather do. She'd always loved animals. "More than people," her dad would joke. She spent most of her spare time lending a hand at Animal Ark with sick cats, dogs, hedgehogs; any animal that needed help. With her shoulder-length blonde hair and slight figure, Mandy could often be spotted around Welford village looking for animals in trouble.

Grandpa stroked Smoky under the chin. "You have a way with them, that's for sure. Doesn't she, Smoky?"

The young gray cat purred his agreement.

"Hardly any time off." Grandma went on pointing out all the minus points about being a vet. "Look at your mom and dad. It's almost Christmas, and they're busier than ever."

Now that the kitchen table was back to normal, Mandy followed her grandma into the living room and helped her lift a big cardboard box full of Christmas decorations down from a closet. She peered inside at the silver baubles and colored lights. "It's because of the cold," she explained. "Animals seem to have more accidents and illnesses this time of year."

"Just like human beings, when you come to think

about it." Grandpa put Smoky down on his favorite red cushion on the sofa and came to help. "Coughs and colds, snuffles and sneezes." He took a tangle of Christmas lights from the box. "That's funny. I'm sure I put these away nice and tidy last year."

Mandy laughed at his puzzled frown. "Should I untangle them for you?" She loved Christmas; putting up the decorations at Animal Ark and Lilac Cottage, making and buying presents. Smoky jumped down from the sofa and came to play. He lifted his paw to bat a light that dangled from Grandpa's hand.

"Yes, please."

So Mandy sat cross-legged on the carpet with Smoky on her lap, patiently untying the knots in the wire until the lights were straightened out, ready for use.

> *"Away in a-a manger,*
> *No-o crib for a bed*
> *The-e little Lord Jesus*
> *La-ay down his sweet head!"*

A carol singer stood at the door.

"Dad!" Mandy recognized the voice. He sang in the church choir. "He must be practicing for a concert."

Smoky cocked an ear, meowed, then crept off under a chair. Grandma and Grandpa laughed.

"We three Kings of Orient are,
One in a taxi, one in a car. . . ."

Grandma dashed to the door to let him in before he had a chance to ruin the song any further. "Adam, come in out of the snow!"

Mandy looked up as he stopped to take off his boots at the door. There were snowflakes in his short brown hair and melting on his beard. He was zipped up inside his winter jacket, blowing warm air into his cold hands. "Did you like my singing?" he said with a grin.

"Fantastic, Dad!"

"What's Smoky doing under there?" He unzipped his jacket and took it off.

"Hiding from the carol singer."

"Hmm. He's got no ear for music, that cat." Mandy's dad settled in a chair by the fire. "Speaking of ears, how is it?"

"Cured, we hope." Mandy handed the lights to her grandpa. "Smoky seems to have stopped scratching already."

"Well done. It gave me time to stop by Bleakfell Hall. I had to check up on Pandora for Mrs. Ponsonby. She has a little chill, that's all. Poor Mrs. P. was worried stiff."

"*Poor Pandora,* you mean!" Grandma didn't always see eye to eye with fussy Mrs. Ponsonby. "That little Pekingese gets carried everywhere. She has no chance to run around and play like any normal dog." She brought in piping hot tea and chocolate cake from the kitchen. "By the way, Adam, did you mention Father Christmas to Mrs. Ponsonby?"

Mandy pricked up her ears.

He snapped his fingers. "No, sorry. I completely forgot."

"Brain like a sieve." Grandma tapped the top of his head. "We need to know if she has room for Rudolph at the Hall."

"What's this?" Mandy was full of curiosity.

Grandma's eyes twinkled. "Rudolph the red-nosed reindeer. You know the tune?"

"Da-dum, de da-da da-dum . . ." Mandy's dad came in with a deep bass version.

"Don't encourage him," Mandy sighed. "Yes, so what about Rudolph and Bleakfell Hall?"

"Father Christmas is going to bring his reindeer to Welford for Christmas Eve!" Grandma announced. "Of course, Rudolph will be a very tired reindeer, coming all the way from Reindeerland. So he'll need a place to stay . . ."

"Oh, Grandma!" Mandy sighed. She knew better than to believe all this stuff. "Everyone knows there's no such . . ."

"Hush. You wash your mouth out with soap and water, Mandy Hope! Father Christmas and his sleigh will be here in person, complete with reindeer. And if you don't believe me, ask your grandpa!"

Mandy looked from one smiling face to another. "Grandpa? . . . Dad?"

They nodded back.

"What's going on?" The grown-ups were up to something. Mandy reached down to pick up Smoky, who'd come creeping close to the warm log fire. She cuddled him to her.

"Father Christmas will make a special guest appearance in the village square this year," was all Grandpa would say. "Everyone's going to be there. Why don't you bring James along and find out?"

James Hunter, Mandy's best friend, lived on the edge of Welford. "Will there really be a reindeer?"

"Two!" Grandma said.

Mandy considered it. "Maybe we will come and have a look." Real reindeer with antlers, trotting through the snow! "Wait a minute, I didn't think there were any reindeer left in this country. Didn't they all die out ages ago?"

"Aha!" Grandpa winked. "But there are plenty in Reindeerland!"

"Anyway," Adam Hope said, "that's where you're wrong. We do have reindeer in Britain. In Scotland, as a matter of fact. They belong to well-managed, domesticated herds in the Cairngorm Mountains. There! *Rangifer tarandus*, to give them their Latin name. They're supervised by the Reindeer Council and looked after by a Mr. Donald McNab."

"Ask me anything you want to know about reindeer!" Grandpa boasted. "For instance, why do reindeer have cloven hooves?"

"I don't know; why *do* reindeer have cloven hooves?" Mandy joined in the fun. It really did seem as if Rudolph was coming for Christmas!

"To help them walk on frozen snow." Grandpa rushed on. "And did you know, a reindeer can pull a sleigh carrying three hundred pounds for a hundred miles a day?"

She shook her head. What was going on? How come they all knew so much about reindeer all of a sudden?

"Stop teasing," Grandma said at last, "and tell poor Mandy why we're all reindeer mad."

"It's all for a good cause," Grandpa explained. "This special guest appearance in the village is in aid of a little girl who lives at Beechtrees. That's the bungalow next to the main road. She and her family came to live in Welford earlier this year. Jeremy Hastings is the new groundsman at the tennis club. Their daughter, Alex, is only five, but they've recently found out that she's seriously ill."

Mandy tried to connect the reindeer's visit with Alex Hastings. She'd seen the girl from a distance — a tiny, red-haired child, with a bigger brother. Their hair was the first thing you noticed about them both. It was curly and shone reddish-gold in the sun. "What's wrong with her?"

"Something to do with her heart. She needs an operation, Mandy dear." Grandma spoke softly, seriously. "There's only one place in the world where she can get this kind of operation, and that's in America. But the Hastings can't afford to take her there. Your grandpa heard about it one day at the tennis club. A few people put their heads together and came up with various ways of raising money so the family could go to the States."

"Fund-raising," Mandy's dad chipped in. "Everyone has been having great ideas. Your grandpa came up with this special invitation to Father Christmas and his reindeer. We hope all of Welford will come along, sing a few carols, and put lots of money in a collection box."

"People have been very good so far," Grandpa said. "We've already raised enough money for the operation,

but we need another eight hundred pounds for the air-
fares to send Alex and her family for treatment. And we
need it quickly. She must go early in the New Year for
the operation, otherwise it'll be too late."

"You mean, if she doesn't get it, she'll die?" Mandy
whispered.

"I'm afraid so, love."

For a while, everyone was silent. The logs crackled in
the hearth, Smoky rubbed his soft face against Mandy's
cheek.

"But if she goes to America and has the operation, the
doctors think she will be completely cured," Grandma
said. "So you see, Father Christmas's visit is going to be
extra-important this year."

Slowly Mandy said, "Does Alex know about going to
America?"

Grandma shook her head. "Her mom and dad think
it's best to keep quiet until they're sure they can take
her. She doesn't really know how ill she is. And she certainly doesn't have a clue about Father Christmas's
visit!"

Adam Hope finished his cup of tea and brushed cake
crumbs from his sweater. Smoky jumped from Mandy's
arms and went to see whether the crumbs were worth
eating. "I saw Alex's dad today, as a matter of fact."

"At Animal Ark?" Mandy found the little girl's story sad but fascinating.

"Yes. He brought a kitten in for her vaccinations. They just got her. Alex loves animals, apparently. Her dad says the walls of her bedroom are plastered with pictures of them!" He glanced at Mandy with a little smile.

"Just like someone else we know!" Grandpa teased. Mandy's own room was a portrait gallery of pets, wild animals, and endangered species.

"Beechtrees is just past Susan Collins's house, isn't it?" Mandy ignored them and got to thinking ahead instead.

"That's right. Why?" Her grandpa bent to plug in the Christmas lights. They lit up, a brilliant chain of blue, green, and pink. "Hey, presto!"

"Oh, nothing . . ." A five-year-old girl with a new kitten! "What's the kitten like?" she asked her dad, as casually as possible.

"She's a little brown-and-black tortoiseshell."

"Sweet!" Mandy stared wistfully at Smoky, now a fully grown cat. "How old?"

"Four or five months, just at the playful stage. You know, she chases everything, including her own tail."

"Aah!"

"And she has the most amazing eyes," her dad continued. "Big and shiny in her cute little dark face."

"What color?" She wanted to picture the kitten perfectly.

"Her eyes? They're a sort of bright gold color. Traffic-light orange. Yes, that's it!" Dr. Adam smiled as he stood up, ready to take Mandy home. He stroked Smoky. "Not as good-looking as you, of course," he said with a grin. "But the Hastings's kitten does have the most amazing amber eyes. And that's what they've called her. Alex chose the name herself; Amber."

They put on their jackets and boots, said good-bye to Mandy's grandparents and Smoky, and began to tramp through the snow up the lane to Animal Ark, Dr. Adam whistling as they walked.

"Dad?"

"What?" He stopped midtune.

"I wonder if I should go and visit Alex and Amber," Mandy said dreamily. There was a white wonderland of snow-laden trees, drifts almost three feet deep against the walls, and stars in a moonlit sky.

"I don't see why not."

"And, Dad . . ."

"Uh-oh!" He gathered snow from the wall top and patted it into shape. His eyes gleamed as he aimed the ball at Mandy. "Come on, this is a challenge!"

"No, Dad, I want to ask you something!" But she

couldn't resist scooping up snow and making her own snowball.

"So I gather. Am I going to say yes? I know you when you give me that look!" He was laughing now, as the first snowball flew toward him. He dodged just in time.

"Listen!" Mandy dived for more ammunition. "You know Grandma thought that the two reindeer might be able to stay at Bleakfell Hall?"

It was her dad's turn to fling a snowball. It thudded against Mandy's shoulder. "Direct hit! Yes, Mrs. Ponsonby has an empty stable at the back of the Hall."

"Well, we could look after them at Animal Ark instead, couldn't we? We've got room in the residential unit. I mean, reindeer aren't all that big!" She stood with her arm raised, fresh snow poised ready.

"Gi-normous!" Dr. Adam dodged and slipped. He landed flat on his back.

Mandy ran over and stood, hands on hips. "But Mrs. Ponsonby wouldn't have a clue how to look after them. We would! You and mom must know all about reindeer."

"Flattery will get you . . . everywhere!" He grinned back up at her.

"You mean yes? The reindeer can stay with us?" She hauled him to his feet.

"For a couple of nights. As long as your mom agrees."

"Yippee!" Mandy charged into a drift and kicked up loose snow. It sprayed up and sparkled. "Oh, Dad, thanks! That's so great." She ran ahead up the lane to Animal Ark. Real reindeer were coming to stay!

Two

"Two reindeer?" Emily Hope was talking on the phone in Reception. Jean Knox, Animal Ark's receptionist, stood listening, her glasses perched high on her forehead. Simon, their nurse, came through from the treatment room, ready for morning office hours. He raised his eyebrows at Mandy when he overheard the conversation.

It was early the next morning; only three days to go until Christmas Eve, and Mandy was keeping her fingers firmly crossed. Her mom had just called the owner of the reindeer herd in Scotland to make arrangements for the visit.

"Rudolph and Dasher?" Dr. Emily smiled. "And you'll bring their food with them?"

Mandy's eyes shone. "We're having two reindeer to stay this Christmas!" she whispered to Simon.

"You must be joking!" Glancing up from the appointment book, he realized that Mandy was serious. "When?"

"Tomorrow, Wednesday."

"How will they travel? By flying over the rooftops?" Simon winked at Jean, who seemed to think that the entire Hope family had finally gone crazy.

"I don't know yet. Hang on a minute." Mandy listened in again.

"We have an open-air compound at the back of Animal Ark, where we exercise the patients. It's small but secure. I think that should be all right. You say the reindeer need to stay out overnight. . . . Yes, OK, someone could meet you in Walton and show you the road over the moor to Welford. It's hard to find if you don't know your way around. . . . We've had snow, but the main roads are fairly clear. Yes, fine."

They waited as arrangements went ahead.

"Tomorrow afternoon? Yes, one of us will be there. We'll meet you outside the bus station in town . . . you should be able to park a trailer there. . . . Just look out for our Animal Ark Land Rover . . . yes, bye, Mr. McNab!" Emily Hope nodded as she put down the phone.

"Correct me if I'm wrong, but did I just hear you break your strictest Animal Ark rule?" Jean asked in disbelief. She'd known the Hopes a long time, and never in living memory had Mandy's mom and dad agreed to let an animal who didn't need treatment come to stay.

"You did." Dr. Emily put on her white coat.

"Here comes our first patient." Mandy hopped off her stool and went to the window. She wanted to change the subject. A car struggled down the lane through the snow.

"Well, I never!" Jean still couldn't believe it.

"They're coming down from a place near Aviemore," Dr. Emily said. "It's quite a journey. Donald McNab is driving down in a trailer . . . to help Father Christmas deliver presents in Welford!"

"Mom!" It looked as if Mandy would have to go along with the Father Christmas thing, though she considered herself much too old.

"What's wrong? You still hang up your stocking for him, don't you?"

"Yes, but . . . oh, OK, you win!" Mandy beamed.

"It's all in a good cause." Her mom explained to Jean the idea behind the reindeer's visit. "We're trying to raise money to send little Alex Hastings to America. You know about her operation, don't you?" Soon everyone in Welford would be in on it, thought Mandy.

"Good idea. I'll be there," Jean promised. "After all, it is Christmas."

"Seven-thirty in the square on Christmas Eve?" Simon asked. "Count me in, too." Mrs. Parker Smythe and her eight-year-old daughter, Imogen, had just come into the clinic. Simon showed them and their pet into a treatment room. "Did you hear about Father Christmas's special visit?" he asked them, as the door swung closed.

"The more the merrier," Emily Hope smiled. She turned to Mandy. "Happy now?"

"I can't wait!"

"Well, why not go and visit Alex, like you planned? I'm sure she could do with some company."

"Now?" Mandy would normally help out in the clinic during vacation.

"Why not? We won't be busy here, not in this weather. And you could tell her there's a special treat in store this Christmas."

"But not exactly what the treat is?" Mandy scrambled out of her white coat and grabbed her jacket.

Dr. Emily put her head to one side, ready to start work. "No," she said. "Let's keep Father Christmas a nice surprise!"

* * *

"Alex likes animals," Mandy promised James. She'd stopped by the Hunters' house, and James had decided to bring his dog, Blackie, along to Beechtrees.

The black Labrador padded through the snow ahead of them, leaving a narrow trail of footprints. When he came to the wide gates of Susan Collins's enormous house, he stopped.

"No, Blackie, that's not where we're going today." James ordered him on. James was dressed for the snow in a padded jacket and a baseball cap. The wind had reddened his cheeks, and his glasses reflected the bright light as he and Mandy loped along after Blackie.

Beechtrees was tucked away under the shadow of some tall trees a few hundred yards down the main road from Susan's house. Today there were few cars on the road; only a yellow snowplow trundling toward them, with Jeremy Hastings sitting at the controls. The plow had been clearing a track from the tennis club toward the main road after the snowfall of the previous night.

"Hello there." Mr. Hastings drew near, then leaned sideways. He was puzzled by the sight of Blackie, James, and Mandy knee-deep in the fresh snow.

"Hello." Mandy knew him as friendly in a quiet sort of

way, never excited or annoyed. She and James had seen him at work around the tennis courts that autumn.

Blackie spoiled the introductions by barking at the snowplow.

"Sorry." James blushed and told him to sit. "He's never seen one close up before."

"That's OK." Jeremy Hastings decided to take a break. He climbed down from the cab. "I know you two, don't I?"

"Yes. I'm James Hunter, and this is Blackie."

"And I'm Mandy Hope." Somehow, because Mr. Hastings was shy, Mandy was self-conscious, too. She felt her face grow hot behind her woollen scarf and hat.

"The vets' daughter?"

She nodded.

"I took Alex's kitten up to Animal Ark for her yesterday. Nice place." He didn't waste words. "Alex doesn't get out much at the moment."

"No. That's why we brought Blackie to see her," James said.

Mandy's blonde hair fell around her face as she took off her hat. "We heard she likes animals."

"She's crazy about them!" For the first time, Jeremy Hastings smiled. "Completely nuts. She'll love you, Blackie. Why don't you all come in?"

Mandy felt that the ice was broken. She grinned at

James and followed the groundskeeper between two tall beech trees, up a path toward the bungalow.

"Alex!" Mr. Hastings opened the door and knocked snow off his boots. "You've got visitors!"

They waited for an answer, but none came.

"She's a little shy with strangers," her father told them. "Hang on a sec." He kicked off his boots and went inside.

"Sit, Blackie." James made him wait on the porch. He and Mandy stared curiously into the hallway.

"What do you want?" a voice challenged from behind them.

They spun around. Blackie jumped up. There in the front garden, peering from behind a bush, was a small boy with bright ginger hair. His eyes were greeny-gray, his face covered in freckles. He wore a navy-blue fleece jacket zipped to his chin and an expression that said, "Get lost!"

"We came to play with Alex," Mandy answered carefully. The boy looked about seven years old.

"Oh, her." He turned away in disgust. "She doesn't want to play." He trudged back onto the lawn and kicked at the deep snow. "I'm her brother, and she won't even play with me."

Mandy couldn't tell who the boy was most angry with, but his tone of voice and his deep frown made her guess that it was everyone and everything. He was what

Grandma would call "moody." That meant he sulked a lot.

"I'll play with you," James volunteered. It was chilly standing on the porch waiting for Alex to appear. "We could build a snowman."

"Where?"

"There on the lawn."

"How tall?"

"As tall as you like."

"Up to the roof of the bungalow?" The boy looked up at the single-story house.

"Well, maybe not that tall." James went ahead anyway. He jumped from the step into the garden and began to scoop snow into a rough pile. "Let's see how fat we can make him."

Mandy pulled her hat from her pocket. "He can wear this when you finish him."

Slowly the boy came and took it. "Can he wear your scarf, too?"

"OK." She unwound it and handed it over.

Satisfied, he ran back to James. Soon they were both hard at work on the snowman's body.

"There, what did I tell you?" Mr. Hastings returned at last, holding his daughter's hand. "Here's a dog that came all this way in the snow to see you. He's called Blackie."

Blackie stood up and wagged his tail at the sound of his name.

Mandy knelt and put an arm around his neck. "He won't bite," she said softly. "He's a nice doggie."

Alex Hastings let go of her father's hand and took a halting step forward. She was small for a five-year-old — pale and thin, wearing a dark blue corduroy dress. Her curly hair was even brighter than Mandy's mom's — the reddest hair that she had ever seen.

Alex's big green eyes grew wide as she reached out a tiny hand to stroke Blackie. "He's all wet!" She took it quickly away.

"That's melted snow. Blackie likes the snow. He tries to eat it!"

Alex stroked him again. "His ears are nice and soft."

"He's one big softie really." Mandy smiled as the little girl grew bolder. "Would your new kitten like to meet him?"

Alex looked up at her dad. "Won't the dog chase Amber?"

"I don't think so. Blackie's probably used to cats. Why don't you get Amber from your bedroom and see?"

As Alex went slowly through one of the doors leading off from the square hallway, Mr. Hastings smiled at Mandy. "Bring Blackie inside and let me close the door.

Alex's mom is fixing hot chocolate for everyone. We could all use some on a day like today."

Mandy smiled back, stepped in, and looked around at the cream-colored walls, the big mirror, and framed family photographs.

"Dad, Amber won't come!" Alex called in a high, panicky voice. "She's hiding under the bed."

There was a faint meow. Blackie pricked up his ears and whined.

"No, she's not! She's running away!"

They heard rapid little feet pattering and jumping

from surface to surface, then a small black-and-brown shape hurtled through the door. The kitten somersaulted into the hall.

"Oh, Amber!" Alex cried from her bedroom.

"It's OK, here she is!" Mr. Hastings cornered the kitten and picked her up.

Mandy held onto Blackie as Alex came slowly over and took Amber from her father. All Mandy could see was a bundle of wriggling fur, a long, fluffy tail, and a little pair of pointed ears. "She's gorgeous!" she exclaimed.

"Amber, be good," Alex scolded. "Say hello to Blackie."

But the kitten caught sight of the big black dog and stared. Her golden eyes flashed, and she opened her mouth wide and hissed.

"No, you have to be nice to him," Alex insisted. She brought her up closer. "Nice doggie. See, Amber; nice, nice doggie!"

Good-natured Blackie sniffed at the kitten. Amber's ears and whiskers twitched. She put out a paw to pat the dog's black nose.

"See, you like him!" Soon it was safe to let go of the kitten. Alex put her on the carpet and watched the two animals stalk in circles around each other. Blackie towered over the kitten, but he was very gentle. Amber, on the other hand, thought that playing meant jumping up at Blackie and catching hold of his neck. She clung on for dear life.

Alex gasped, then laughed. "They're playing a game!"

Mandy told her all about Blackie and James. "James is my best friend. He helps us with the animals at Animal Ark." She explained that her mom and dad looked after sick animals.

Alex didn't take her eyes off Amber and Blackie. "Are they all sick?" she asked slowly.

"Who, the patients who come to my house?" Mandy nodded. "But most of them get better. It's like a hospital for animals."

The little girl turned to her with a serious face. "I've been to the hospital."

"I know," Mandy said gently.

"I might have to go again, so they can make me better. Then I can play outside with William."

"That's her brother," Mr. Hastings explained.

"I know. We met him in the garden. James is out there building a snowman with him." Mandy took Alex to the glass door to look outside. The snowman was already as high as William's shoulder.

"Who's building a snowman?" Alex's mother popped her head around the kitchen door.

"William and James." Alex peered out wistfully at the

snow scene. Then she turned her attention back to the two animals. "Amber's got a friend," she told her mom.

Mrs. Hastings stepped into view. She was small and neat, in dark pants and a soft, fawn-colored sweater. Her short hair was a darker red than her children's, with rich coppery tints.

She smiled at Mandy. "So have you," she said to her daughter. "A new friend. What a lovely surprise!"

Mandy was soon made welcome in the Hastings's house. Alex took her and Blackie into her bedroom. From there they could see James and William out in the garden. The snowman was growing; he had a head and a face made from twigs and stones.

"What's Father Christmas bringing you?" Alex sat on her bed with Amber on her lap. Surrounded by pillows and cushions, she looked like a little red-haired doll.

"I'm not sure." Mandy smiled.

"Do you believe in him?" Alex asked solemnly. She didn't give Mandy a chance to reply. "I do! I wrote to him with a list of things."

"What did you ask for?"

"Well, it's not things exactly. Anyway, I can't tell. It's a secret. Otherwise it won't come true, like a wish."

Beneath the cheerful chatter, Mandy suspected that Alex was sad. From the way she sat stroking her kitten, she could even imagine what Alex's wish might have been. "Dear Father Christmas, Please give me an operation to make me better, so I can go out and play."

"Do you like reindeer?" Alex chatted on. "I do! My favorite is Rudolph. Who's your favorite?"

Mandy glanced up at the giant color pictures of kittens and puppies, ponies, and hamsters. She could hardly see a square inch of bare wall space. "Rudolph." She bit her lip. Sometimes it was difficult not to spill the beans. Little did Alex know it, but she was about to get a visit from her favorite reindeer!

"Poor Rudolph, he couldn't join in any reindeer games, could he?" Alex sighed.

"Because his nose was too red. They didn't like him," Mandy reminded her.

"I would have let him join in anyway."

"Me, too." Mandy sat on the floor with Blackie, happy to talk to Alex as if Rudolph was a real, live reindeer. Alex seemed to know the story inside out.

"Why did it matter what color his nose was?" Alex was determined to stick up for Santa's problem solver. "When I'm better, anyone who wants to can play with me! I'll go back to school, and *everyone* can be my friend!"

Mandy agreed. Suddenly, there was a loud thud

against the window. They turned quickly, in time to see a flattened snowball sliding down the glass.

"William!" Alex gasped. The windowpane had rattled. Startled, Amber had jumped from her lap and gone into hiding. Blackie gave a sharp bark.

"Alex, come and look!" The boy's voice from the garden was high and bossy. Another snowball landed against the glass.

Slowly Alex uncrossed her legs. Mandy helped her from the bed. She could only move at a snail's pace, Mandy realized, and was quickly out of breath.

"Come here. Look at this!"

From the window, the girls could see two snowmen. One wore Mandy's red-and-white-striped hat and scarf. The other had James's cap perched on his head.

"What's going on in here?" Mrs. Hastings came rushing into the room with a worried frown. She glanced at the melting snowballs sliding slowly down the windowpane. "What was that noise?"

"William's snowballs. Look what they built in the garden!" Alex's face was bright with admiration.

But Mrs. Hastings was annoyed as she came to the window.

From outside, William saw his mother and yelled. "Mom, look!" He sounded faint through the glass, but they could tell he was proud of the snowmen. "Can Alex come out and see?"

Mrs. Hastings tapped hard on the window. "No, she can't!" she mouthed. "And you come inside at once!"

Mandy saw the smile vanish from William's face. James stood by, unsure.

"Alex, it's time for your medicine," her mother said sharply. Frowning, she left the room to get it.

"William's going to get it now," Alex whispered. "He's not supposed to do things that make me jump." She sighed and retreated to her bed. "Now he'll think it's my fault that he's in trouble again."

"Oh, I'm sure he won't," Mandy began. But she heard doors bang and Mrs. Hastings's voice speaking to her son.

". . . No consideration . . . making loud noises . . . you are seven years old; old enough to know better, William!"

Alex hung her head and put her hands over her ears.

"We'd better go," Mandy said quickly. James still stood out there in the cold.

Alex nodded. "I have to have a nap after my medicine anyway." She blushed and smiled. "Thanks for bringing Blackie to see me."

"Thanks for showing me Amber." The kitten peeped out from under the bed, her eyes shining big and golden. "Enjoy the snowmen!" Alex would be able to see them from her bed. Mandy smiled again and left.

Outside, she found James waiting for her, and, at the gate, the worried figure of Jeremy Hastings.

"Alex has to be kept nice and quiet," he said to explain Mrs. Hastings's anger about the snowballs. "No exertion. It's doctors' orders. Of course, if she gets her operation, it'll be a different story. She'll be running around just like she was before."

"Grandpa says the fund-raising is going really well," Mandy said.

He nodded and smiled grimly. "A lot depends on this Father Christmas thing."

"Don't worry. It'll be amazing; a sleigh, real reindeer — Alex will love it!"

"You didn't mention it to her?"

"No." It had been hard, but Mandy had kept the secret.

"Good. It's bound to cheer her up, isn't it?" Mr. Hastings gazed up at the trees, as if he would find an answer there to his family's problems. "Alex has always loved Father Christmas and his reindeer."

Mandy and James said good-bye. They left Mr. Hastings standing by his snowplow, gazing up at the gray sky.

Three

"I'm sorry I'm late." Donald McNab strolled up to the Animal Ark Land Rover.

It was just before dinner the next day, and Mandy and James had driven into Walton with Dr. Adam to meet their special guests. After an hour of sitting freezing in the car, with James snuffling and sneezing into his hankie, Mandy's dad had hurried off to buy warm drinks. It had been a long, cold wait.

"Aye, I lost my way," the Scotsman explained in a heavy accent. He sounded very calm. "Took a couple of wrong turnings in York. Terrible place to drive through.

I went around the old city walls three times before I found the right exit. My head was spinning by the time I got out."

"That's OK." Mandy and James looked eagerly for the reindeer in Mr. McNab's trailer, which he'd parked a few yards up the road. They weren't interested in why he was late.

"I thought maybe I'd missed you." He shook hands as first James, then Mandy jumped down onto the pavement. His gray eyes shone with good humor, his handshake was firm. "It was good of you to wait."

"Dad won't be long," Mandy said. "Mr. McNab, can we go and take a look?" All day she'd been looking forward to this.

"At Rudolph and Dasher? Aye, go right ahead. And call me Don!" He fished deep in the pocket of his weatherproof jacket. "Here, you can give them a wee treat for being cooped up in that trailer for so long."

They took a handful each of what looked suspiciously like scraps of chewed leather. James sniffed them and wrinkled his nose.

"Dried mushrooms," Don laughed. "They love 'em!"

Mandy couldn't wait a moment longer. She ran ahead. From inside the gray trailer came a loud shuffling and knocking of hooves. She saw that the back doors were half open, like stable doors, and as she drew near, two heads loomed out; two long noses, two pairs of dark brown eyes, and two sets of enormous antlers.

Mandy held her breath. The animals were only the height of a small Welsh pony, but their antlers were huge, branching off like mighty boughs on a tree. They curved over the reindeer's heads as they nodded and poked them out of the trailer.

"Go ahead!" Don encouraged. "They won't harm you!"

Gingerly, Mandy reached up with the mushrooms. The nearest reindeer bent to nibble at them with his velvety mouth.

"That's Dasher."

James followed suit, letting the other reindeer take food from his palm.

"And that's Rudolph. Say hello, boys!"

The reindeer snorted and grunted. The trailer shook as they shifted their weight.

By now a small crowd had gathered. Walton had never seen a reindeer in the flesh. Word went around for people to come and look at their magnificent antlers. Mothers came with children, shopkeepers stood out on the pavement. One bus driver even stopped his bus to let his passengers see, while Don McNab fielded eager questions.

"They
plai
sk

ve come to help Father Christmas," he ex-
ed to the smallest children. "They have to pull his
igh through the snow."

"When?"

"Where?"

"Will we see them?" More questions, more round eyes and open mouths.

"Aye, you will if you come to Welford on Christmas Eve," Don told them. "That's when the old gentleman will bring your presents!" He winked at James and Mandy.

Through all the fuss, Rudolph and Dasher chewed contentedly, until Adam Hope came back with the drinks and the children had to say good-bye.

"Do you think you'll be able to follow us OK?" Mandy's dad asked Don after the two men had met.

But Mandy came up with a better idea. She arranged to drive with Don in the reindeer van. "Just in case they can't keep up," she explained.

"Och aye, I don't want to get lost again!" Don helped her into the passenger seat. All the way home, out of town and across the moor, Mandy was able to fire questions at him.

"What do reindeer eat?" she asked, hoping she'd be able to help feed them later.

"Grass, moss, ferns, bark, oh aye, and mushrooms, of course," Don answered, as he drove carefully down the hill toward Welford. The whole valley lay under a blanket of snow, and the village lights twinkled in the dusk. He stifled a yawn. "I'm away to my bed early tonight."

Mandy smiled happily. "We'll take care of the reindeer for you," she promised.

"Aye, I know you will. Anyhow, I've a busy day tomorrow."

It would be Thursday tomorrow, the day before Christmas Eve. "Where do you have to go?" Mandy asked.

"I've to drive the reindeer to a children's hospital in Leeds tomorrow morning. The old gentleman will be handing out presents there."

Mandy shot a puzzled look at the cheerful little Scotsman. He had short gray hair, a square face, a nice, outdoorsy feel. "This old gentleman . . ." she began.

"Father Christmas, aye?"

"I mean, aren't you . . . Isn't it really . . . ?" She stammered to a halt. Here was another grown-up who liked to tease.

"Me?" He roared with laughter and thumped the steering wheel. "Oh, no, dearie! Don't ever let him catch you saying such a thing, or there'll be no presents for you this year!"

He went on chuckling as they followed Dr. Adam and James through the village, past the pub and the post office, along the lane to Animal Ark.

Four

"Hold him steady," Don told Mandy as she led Rudolph down the ramp from the trailer into the yard.

The reindeer tossed his head and pawed the ground stiffly until he grew used to his new surroundings.

"Here come the guests of honor." Emily Hope stood on the doorstep after evening office hours.

"They're . . . awesome!" Simon gave a low whistle. "Look at those antlers!"

Rudolph grunted suspiciously, then allowed Mandy to lead him on. She took him around the back to the residential area and gave him a reward. "Good boy." She stroked his thick white winter mane.

"Steady as you go." Don steered James and Dasher down the ramp. He took a look at the high wire fence surrounding the exercise compound. "Aye, this'll do nicely."

Mandy breathed a sigh of relief. The reindeer's long journey had ended safely. "Will they need food?" she asked Don, anxious again as Rudolph and Dasher began to paw at the snow. "They must be hungry."

"No need. They can dig, see."

The reindeer lowered their heads and began to scrape with their antlers, using them as giant snow shovels. Soon they were down to green grass and grazing happily.

Mandy, James, Adam and Emily Hope, Simon, and Jean all gathered around to watch. "They don't seem to mind an audience," Dr. Adam said quietly.

"Och, they're used to it. They're at the center of the action wherever they go." Don went to fetch his own bag from the battered white van. He looked up at the soft snowflakes floating out of the dark sky. "Good reindeer weather. It reminds them of home."

"Come inside and get warm." Unless there was an emergency call during the evening, Emily Hope had finished work for the day. She took Don's bag and carried it into the house. Simon and Jean went inside to clean up the clinic.

"Aye, in a wee while." Don grinned at Mandy and James. "I just want to show these two the sleigh belonging to the old gentleman himself!" He stayed out in the yard as the other grown-ups went indoors.

James and Mandy shrugged and followed.

"But it's the trailer!" James was disappointed. Father Christmas's sleigh was just like any other trailer that you would see on a farm or at a horse show.

"Not just any ordinary trailer, young Jim!" Don McNab leaped into action. He unscrewed nuts and bolts, removed the detachable roof, folded down fiberglass flaps, and soon transformed the trailer into what looked for all the world like an old-fashioned sleigh.

"Wow!" James was impressed. The painted side panels hid the wheels and looked like imitation sleigh runners.

"Abracadabra! We hitch the reindeer onto the front, and jingle bells, off we go!"

"That's really neat," Mandy said.

"Aye, it is."

"Who thought of it?" James tipped his glasses more firmly on to his nose and went to inspect it more closely.

"I did." Don was proud of his handiwork. "I use it to tour the country at Christmastime. In two shakes I can turn the trailer into the old gentleman's sleigh. He arrives in style to visit the kiddies in the hospital or turn on the Christmas lights, whatever they want."

"I like it!" James examined the hinges and molded fiberglass and the metal shafts that harnessed the reindeer.

"Then why not come with us tomorrow?" Don promptly invited them both along. "We're off to visit the little kids in the hospital in Leeds. You two can keep me on the right road." He reminded them how hopeless he was at finding his way.

"Great; we could help look after Rudolph and Dasher!" Mandy jumped at the chance. She ran inside to ask her mom and dad.

"Yes, fine," Emily Hope said. She stood by the stove in the warm kitchen. "Would you tell Don that supper's ready?"

They sat down to steaming bowls of thick soup and piles of fresh bread. Don McNab ate with a ravenous appetite, entertaining them with stories of the reindeer herd at home. Mandy lapped it all up; the rolling sound of the Scotsman's voice, the picture he painted of snowy mountains and magnificent animals.

Before she went to bed, Mandy went outside to check one last time on Rudolph and Dasher. They were still happily shoveling snow with their antlers to reach the grass. Tomorrow, Mandy and James would go with them to visit the children in the hospital. The day after would be Grandpa's fund-raising event for Alex. Mandy sighed and let the light snowflakes settle on her nose. This was going to be the most exciting Christmas ever!

"Two days to go before I open my stocking!" Simon rubbed his hands as he came in the next morning. He was wearing layers of sweaters under his jacket, and a woolly hat was pulled down over his forehead. Outside, it was sunny but freezing cold.

Mandy had been up bright and early, along with her parents, while their Scottish guest slept in. She'd already answered the phone to half a dozen worried pet owners. The appointment book was full.

"Just think, back home for Christmas Day; sleeping in, presents, turkey, and Christmas pudding!" Simon put on his white coat.

"Can we fit Mr. Pickard in?" Mandy ran her finger down the list of appointments. Walter was on the phone to say that his old cat, Tom, was under the weather.

Simon nodded. "We'll squeeze him in, but don't tell Jean."

So Mandy made the appointment. "He'd like to come in right away. He sounds worried."

And that was the start of a pre-Christmas rush at Animal Ark. At half-past eight, Jean arrived and took over for Mandy at the desk. Mandy put on her white coat, ready to help her mom and dad. There were three dogs, two cats, a hamster, and a hedgehog to feed and clean.

And of course, there were Rudolph and Dasher to see to. As she went out with a special mix of oats and molasses recommended by Don, the reindeer raised their heads in greeting. Dasher trotted right over to his dish of cereal and began to eat, but Rudolph took one sniff at his and turned up his nose. *That's strange*, Mandy thought. She patted his shaggy neck, frowned, and went back inside.

Then there was a waiting room full of patients, with old Walter Pickard and Tom at the front of the line. Mandy was on hand as they came into Dr. Adam's treatment room.

"Let's take a look at this old fellow." Mandy's dad waited for Walter to lift Tom out of his basket.

Tom appeared, sad and bedraggled. Normally a sturdy, heavyweight cat, black and white, barrel-shaped, with a black patch of fur over one eye, today he looked thin and ill. He snuffled, his head hung low, his eyes dull.

Adam Hope examined his eyes and throat. "Has he been eating properly?"

Walter shook his head. "He's stopped eating his grub. It's not like Tom."

"Has he been sneezing? Coughing?" Dr. Adam beckoned Mandy to take a look. "See these little ulcers on his tongue?"

She nodded. "Is it cat flu?"

"It looks like it." He took Tom's temperature and confirmed that it was high.

Walter sighed. The old man treated Tom as a companion. Like him, the cat was a tough customer, but getting on in years. And this year, Walter had forgotten to have him vaccinated. "Can you do anything for him?"

Dr. Adam stroked Tom. "He'll need antibiotics to treat any secondary infection and plenty of fluids, but you should be able to take him home and nurse him there. You'll have to keep him warm. Clean up his eyes and nostrils if they get blocked. Poor old guy, he's having trouble breathing."

"He's feeling sorry for himself all right."

Dr. Adam decided to dose Tom with antibiotics there and then. Mandy helped to hold the cat, as her father showed Walter the best way to get the syrup down his throat. "Remember, this is a viral infection," he explained. "You'll have to wash Tom's bedding and feeding bowls, then disinfect them. Don't let him near other cats, OK?"

Walter promised to take good care of him. "Thank

you, Dr. Hope," he said meekly, as he put Tom back in his basket.

"Give us a call to let us know how he's getting along with the medicine. And don't worry, we'll soon have him back on his feet, terrorizing the neighborhood again!"

The old man smiled weakly. "I hope you're right." He shuffled out of the room with his pet.

Dr. Adam glanced at Mandy. "And don't you worry! Tom will be fine."

"It's not that." Mandy frowned. "It's Rudolph." She remembered that he too had sounded chesty when she took out the dish of food. And he had the look that Tom had come in with — dull-eyed and moping. She told her dad how the reindeer had turned down the oats.

"Hmm. Do you want me to take a look?"

Though the waiting room was full to overflowing, Mandy nodded.

"Come on then, quick!"

They went out together into the snowy compound, where the difference between the two reindeer was now quite clear. Dasher, whom Mandy recognized by his shorter antlers and dark coat, came trotting nimbly, hooves clicking. But Rudolph kept his distance and gazed listlessly. When Mandy and Adam Hope ap-

proached him, he simply lowered his head and sat down in the snow.

"Not so good." Adam Hope frowned. "It looks like you were right, Mandy. We may have a sick reindeer on our hands."

They examined Rudolph and brought Don out to look. Dr. Adam diagnosed a viral infection that needed the kind of treatment he'd prescribed for Tom. "Plenty of food, plenty of water. Keep him separate from Dasher."

Don nodded. He had talked Rudolph back onto his feet and stood patting his neck.

"He should be over it in a day or two. Perhaps even in time for Christmas. It's a kind of twenty-four hour reindeer flu."

But this left Don with a problem. "I can't let the kiddies down this morning," he told them.

"Can Dasher pull the sleigh by himself?" Mandy asked.

"He can manage it if Father Christmas walks alongside instead of sitting on top. You think I should go ahead and leave Rudolph behind to recover?"

"I'll stay here to look after him!" Mandy promised.

So when James arrived, with a cold but ready for the trip into Leeds, he and Don led Dasher into the trailer and prepared to set off alone.

"You're sure you don't mind, Mandy?" James asked.

"No. We're really busy at the clinic in any case. I'll be more use staying here."

"Aye, you look after Rudolph." Don sat at the wheel, ready to move off.

". . . the red-nosed reindeer!" James grinned.

"Ha-ha!" She grinned back. "Don't get lost!" she called, as the van and trailer eased out of the yard.

"Very funny!" James leaned out and waved a map. "Don't worry, we'll be back by dinner!"

"Mandy!" Jean called her inside. "Would you mind manning the telephone for the next hour? The clinic is running late, and I did promise that I'd dash into the village to meet Lydia Fawcett for coffee. I tried to ring High Cross to cancel it, but she'd already left."

Mandy agreed willingly. She took over in Reception, seeing the last patients into the treatment rooms and answering the busy phone. Every now and then she would glance out at Rudolph. He seemed the same — no better, no worse.

"Welford 703267, Animal Ark!" She picked up the phone. It was nearly lunchtime. Her dad had gone out on an emergency call to Sam Western's dairy herd at Upper Welford Hall. Her mom was busy treating patients in the unit.

"Hello?" A woman's voice hesitated. "This may not be the right thing to do, but I wondered if you could give me some advice?"

"Mrs. Hastings?" Mandy recognized the voice. "Is it something to do with Amber?" Her first thought was that the kitten might have developed a case of cat flu, like Walter's Tom.

"Oh, hello, Mandy. Actually it is. It's OK, she's not ill. It's nothing like that."

Mandy was relieved but puzzled.

"It's a silly thing in a way . . ."

"Shall I fetch Mom?"

"No, I really don't want to bother her. Perhaps you could help. You see, Amber's been really naughty this morning. She was in a mischievous mood, playing hide-and-seek. Anyway, Alex lost her. We looked, but we couldn't find her anywhere inside the house. But when my husband came home for lunch a few minutes ago, he saw where Amber was." Mrs. Hastings paused for breath.

"Where?" Mandy pictured the garden path, the porch, the single-story building.

"On the roof! I went out to look, and there she was, the naughty little thing, perched halfway up, refusing to come down!"

"Do you think she's stuck?"

"We don't know. Jeremy says that if she managed to get up, surely she can manage to get down. He thinks we should wait and see."

Mandy knew that cats, even kittens of Amber's age, had excellent balance. On the other hand, it must be very cold up there on the roof. "Have you tried to tempt her down?"

"Yes. I've just put out a saucer of milk on the front step. We've been calling her, but she takes no notice. What do you think we should do?"

"Keep trying," Mandy decided. "Try some food as well

as the milk. And tell Alex that cats usually come down when they're ready."

"All right." Mrs. Hastings sounded reassured. "It's just that at the moment we don't like anything to upset Alex. But anyway, you're probably right. We'll try the food, Mandy. Thank you very much."

"That's OK. Will you call us when Amber comes down?" Mandy would be uneasy until the problem was solved. She put down the phone and checked with Simon that she'd done the right thing.

"Fine," he confirmed. He brought a list of things for Mandy to do. "Can you help me put a fresh dressing on the cocker spaniel's leg? Then we have to fit a cone collar to the border collie."

"To stop him from biting his stitches?" The farm dog had a jagged wound on his back. The collar made a cone shape around the dog's head so that he couldn't turn and tug at the affected area.

Simon nodded. They went ahead with the routine tasks. Then, in the middle of the afternoon, Emily Hope popped her head around the door to check in with them. She looked busy but perfectly in control. The phone rang again. "Get that, Mandy, would you?"

Mandy dashed into Reception. Perhaps it was Lisa Hastings with good news about Amber. "Welford 703267."

"Hi, Mandy, it's me!" James sounded far-off. "Listen, you'll never guess what happened."

"Hi, James. You got lost?"

"No. We found the hospital OK. Father Christmas did his bit even though I didn't actually see it. The nurses said my cold made me infectious. Anyway, all the kids got their presents. Dasher went into the ward with him. They loved it."

"So?" She leaned sideways to look out of the window for a quick check on Rudolph.

"We're snowed in."

"What?" Her jaw dropped.

"We're stuck here in Leeds. It's snowing like crazy, the roads are blocked, and we can't move!"

"Oh, no!" If they didn't get back before tomorrow, this would turn into a major crisis. "For how long?"

"No one knows. They're out with the snowplow and salt trucks, but you should see it, Mandy! People are saying that it might go on all day and all night!"

"Where are you exactly?"

"We're still at the hospital. Don was able to put Dasher out on the lawn, so he's happy. But he figures we might not get back to Welford tonight."

"What about tomorrow?" Christmas Eve; Father Christmas's special appearance. The collection for Alex. Her operation! Mandy's heart sank.

"We don't know. We hope we can make it. Don says to keep our fingers crossed. He said to ask how Rudolph is."

"He's OK. He still looks down in the dumps, though. Listen, James . . ."

"Quick, Mandy. My money's running out."

The phone line crackled. "What are we going to do if you don't make it?"

Bip-bip-bip! The line buzzed and went dead. Mandy put down the phone with an empty click. She almost panicked. What a day! One crisis after another. And now, with just twenty-four hours to go to the big event, they had no sleigh, just one sick reindeer, and no Father Christmas!

Five

"Mandy, what on earth's the matter?" Her grandpa strode into the clinic in his walking boots, thick socks, and a down jacket. He was on his way to the village and had stopped by to see if they needed anything from the general store.

"Oh, Grandpa; Father Christmas — Don McNab — is snowed in. He might not be able to get back for tomorrow night!"

"Well, I never!" Even Tom Hope was thrown for a loop. "But we've already told everyone to come. They're even coming in from Walton to see him. They're expecting us to put on a good show." He sat for a moment on a chair in the waiting room. He took off his thick gloves and ran a hand through his gray hair. "And we're relying on that collection money to raise the final eight hundred pounds."

"I know." Mandy began to think. She stopped panicking, determined not to look on the bad side. "If worse comes to worst, at least we'll still have Rudolph."

"But no sleigh and no Father Christmas," Grandpa groaned.

"No, and I suppose we don't even know if Rudolph will be better in time." Mandy's nerve faltered as she glanced outside. It was the darkest time of the year. The light was already fading from an overcast sky. But at least it wasn't snowing here in Welford, and Rudolph was starting to scrape away at the snow to find the greenest grass shoots. "But let's say he does make it," she went on. "Dad said it might be a twenty-four hour thing."

"Yes?" Grandpa looked weary. "All that planning, and it could come to nothing," he mumbled.

"Listen!" Mandy went and crouched beside him, willing him not to give in. "Rudolph looks OK; at least we'll have one reindeer!"

"And one is better than none?"

"Yes, and maybe the sleigh isn't that important. Or maybe someone like Mr. Western or Mr. Collins could lend us a trailer. We could decorate it with Christmas lights to make it look like a sleigh!"

"A do-it-yourself effort?" Grandpa perked up.

"Yes!" There was no stopping Mandy now. "Ernie Bell's good at making things. Maybe we could get him to help. And it would be easy to get a substitute Father Christmas. All we need is a big red suit with a hood and some white fur trimming. A big white beard, a sackful of presents . . ." Her imagination ran on.

"And someone to wear it," Grandpa reminded her.

"Yes." She stopped and looked him in the eye. "Grand . . ."

"Oh, well, I don't know about that." He coughed and stood up. "I don't know that I'd be any good at dressing up. But you're right about the rest, Mandy. What we have to do now is mention it to a few people. I'm sure someone will volunteer right away!"

". . . I'll think about it." Julian Hardy, the landlord at the Fox and Goose, listened to Grandpa and Mandy's request. "It's kind of short notice, but I'll consider it."

They'd left Animal Ark and walked into the village to look for a substitute Father Christmas. The landlord was an obvious choice. The plan was for the procession to start outside the pub with traditional carols and the collection, before it moved up the road to Beechtrees.

"Come on, Dad!" John Hardy encouraged him to be a good sport. "They need someone to say yes right now."

"Ho-ho-ho!" The landlord practiced his laugh. "No, it's not me," he said with a frown. "Besides, we'll be busy in the pub."

"Oh, Dad!"

"Let me think about it." This was his final word for now, so Mandy and Tom Hope continued across the square to Walter Pickard's corner house.

". . . Me, dress up as Father Christmas?" Walter snorted. He'd invited them into his kitchen, but now he evidently wished he hadn't. "I never heard anything so silly!"

"Wait a minute. Think about it." Grandpa Hope stood there, perfectly reasonable. "You're the right age for the job, Walter."

"And so are you," he retorted.

"Yes, but I'm more on the management side of things. I'm a behind-the-scenes kind of guy."

Walter's eyebrows shot up. "Oh, really?"

"Yes. Whereas you're more the hands-on sort. I can just see you in a Father Christmas outfit, Walter. Besides, you wouldn't want to let everyone down, would you?"

Walter hemmed and hawed. He coughed and shuffled. He said his rheumatism was bad, Tom was sick and needed full-time care.

"Then you won't be in the Fox and Goose for a pint tonight?" Grandpa said with a sly wink at Mandy.

"Oh, I don't know about that," came the instant response. He glowered at his visitors, unable to turn them down flat. "I'll think about it," he said as he showed them to the door. "I'll mention it to Ernie. He's more your man!"

". . . Father Christmas?" Adam Hope considered it. "I'm a little on the young side, aren't I?"

They'd bumped into him outside the post office on his way back from Sam Western's place. Customers came and went, rushing in to mail late Christmas cards and out again to do last-minute errands. Dr. Adam had stopped the Land Rover to offer Mandy and her grandfather a lift.

"I don't mind calling Sam Western to ask if we can borrow his trailer," he told them when he heard about the crisis. "But I'm not so sure about playing the old man."

"You'd be good at it," Mandy pleaded. "Wouldn't he, Grandpa?"

"Perfect. Just the right, friendly sort of fellow." But it looked as if Grandpa Hope was beginning to think he would have to do the job himself after all. "Look, if no one else wants to, I suppose I could go home and get an outfit together before tomorrow night. . . ."

"I might be out on call. Anything could happen between now and then." Mandy's dad certainly wouldn't commit himself. "Nice try, Mandy. I'll think about it."

"What's the problem?" A familiar voice interrupted. Mrs. Ponsonby appeared at the post office door, ready to step into any breach. "Do I take it that the real Father Christmas has disappeared?" She chortled at Mandy as she descended onto the pavement.

Mandy swallowed hard. Given half a chance, Mrs. Ponsonby would step in and start bossing them around. "He's stuck in Leeds," she admitted. "It's still snowing there. The roads are blocked."

"Oh, dearie me!" And take charge Mrs. Ponsonby did, standing there on the pavement with her two dogs, Toby and Pandora, both dressed in their little tartan jackets. "We must do something!" She braced herself. The feathers in her red hat blew in the chilly breeze. Her round figure stood firm. "We must find another!"

"Which is exactly what we're trying to do." Mandy's grandpa tried to get a word in.

Mrs. Ponsonby swatted him away with her hand. "Hush, Tom, I'm thinking. . . . Yes, of course! Now look, you just leave it all to me!"

*   *   *

When Mandy and her grandfather had done everything they could in the village, they went back to Animal Ark. It was late, so Grandpa continued down the lane to Lilac Cottage to hatch his own plans, while Mandy went into the house, tired and hungry.

"Which do you want first, the good news or the bad news?" her mom asked.

"The good news." Mandy sighed and kicked off her boots. "Please, tell me that it's stopped snowing in Leeds and the roads are clear. Don is on his way back."

"If only." Emily Hope gave her a quick hug. "But Rudolph is definitely on the mend. His temperature's down and he's eating normally."

"Thank heavens for that." Now the Christmas procession wouldn't be a complete flop. Rudolph could be the star of the show.

"Rudolph saves the day, just like in the song." Adam Hope was on the phone. "I'm calling Susan Collins's dad to arrange for him to bring his trailer over first thing in the morning."

"So what's the bad news?" Mandy asked warily. Her mom was dressed to go out into the snow in her hat and jacket.

"I just heard from Lisa Hastings at Beechtrees. Amber's still up on the roof."

"Oh, no! Didn't the food tempt her down?"

"Apparently not. And the temperature's dropped below freezing again. I said I'd go over to see if there was anything I could do."

"I'll come!" Though she was exhausted, Mandy immediately offered to help.

"Good. Come on, then. The sooner the better."

So Mandy turned around, stuck her feet back into her boots, and went with her mom.

"Tiring day?" Dr. Emily drove confidently down the narrow lane. The snow sparkled yellow under the headlights. When her four-wheel drive caught a low branch or a bush, a shower of soft snow fell to the ground.

Mandy nodded. "Poor Amber. She's been up there for hours."

"I know. And it's turned very cold again. I'm worried about hypothermia." She glanced at Mandy. "When body temperature falls below a certain level in an animal, or a person for that matter, it makes the victim sleepy. If it's bad, they become unconscious."

"And Amber's only a kitten."

"That makes it worse, I'm afraid. Kittens are more susceptible. They don't have as much body fat to protect them against the cold."

Mandy bit her lip and tried not to think that far ahead.

Beechtrees came into sight as they drove past the Collinses' house. The main road was busy with traffic driving home from work or from last-minute Christmas shopping in Walton. Soon the car pulled up outside the bungalow.

"There she is; she's still up there!" Mandy scrambled out of the car as she spotted a tiny dark shape on the long slope of the white roof. Mr. Hastings stood in the front yard. A ladder leaned against the side of the house.

"Let's hope it's not too late." Emily Hope carried her heavy vet's bag to the porch. She had a quick word at the door with Mrs. Hastings.

"We're sorry to drag you out," Alex's mother began, "but we've tried everything, short of actually climbing onto the roof. It's very slippery. And besides, Jeremy's afraid that it would scare the kitten even higher and make her lose her balance."

"We don't mind." Dr. Emily gave a reassuring smile. "Where's Alex?"

"She's in her room. She's worried sick about poor Amber. No one knows how the kitten got onto the roof, but Alex is convinced it's her fault for not taking better care of her. She's crying her eyes out."

"Tell her to try not to worry." Emily Hope stepped back from the porch and together with Mandy went to join Mr. Hastings at the foot of the ladder.

"It's no good." He shook his head. "Every time I climb up there, she just creeps farther away. I don't want to scare her into making a false move."

Mandy craned her neck to see the tiny kitten. She could just make out a sorry bundle of fur shivering on the roof. She heard a feeble meow. Amber was too frightened to move a muscle.

"How cold will she be up there?" Mr. Hastings asked, anxious but helpless.

"Very cold. She'll get frostbite if she has to stay any longer." Dr. Emily made a quick decision. "Mandy and I will take a shot at getting Amber down, but meanwhile I think you should call the SPCA. They have the right equipment to get up there. Explain the situation to them, and see if they can come out right away!"

He nodded and ran inside. As he opened the door, Mandy caught a glimpse of William hovering in the hall-way. It seemed he was curious to know what was going on but was also trying to keep out of the way. The door closed again and shut him inside.

"Let me go up the ladder, Mom," Mandy said quickly. "Amber knows me. She's more likely to come when I get up there and call her."

Emily Hope checked the ladder. "OK, but don't try anything risky when you get up there. I don't want you climbing onto the roof under any circumstances. Got that?" She knew Mandy would be willing to risk it unless she ordered her not to.

Mandy had to agree. She would have to rely on coaxing Amber down.

"Good luck," her mom said, holding the ladder firm as Mandy set her foot on the first metal rung.

She counted the steps; six, seven, eight. At nine, her head reached roof level. She peered up the snowy slope to the ridge. Amber sat and shivered against the chimney. Her eyes gleamed orange in the dark. "Here, Amber!" Mandy edged up another rung. The kitten backed away.

"That's far enough, Mandy!" her mom warned from below. "If she won't come when you call, we'll leave it to the SPCA!"

Mandy leaned against the gutter and reached out with both hands. Her legs had begun to tremble. The icy wind whipped up loose snow and blew it in her face. "Amber, don't be scared. Come this way!"

In her confusion, Amber thought that Mandy's outstretched arms meant danger. She edged back again, almost lost her footing on the snow-covered ridge, and half slipped from sight. Mandy gasped. With a struggle, the kitten found her balance and cowered against the chimney.

"Any good?" Dr. Emily called.

"No!" Mandy looked desperately along the treacherous surface. The roof was smooth and white except for two raised squares where windows had been built in for extra light. These, too, were snow-covered, but they gave Mandy an idea. "I'm coming down!" Forcing her trembling legs into action, she climbed down the ladder.

"What next?" Emily Hope looked at her watch. "Where's the SPCA?"

"I'm going to try from inside!" Mandy ran to explain to Mr. and Mrs. Hastings. "Can you open the roof windows from inside the house?"

Jeremy Hastings nodded. "They work on hinges and lift up. Come and see!"

He led her to Alex's bedroom.

"Mandy, please get Amber down!" The little girl sat huddled on her bed, crying at the thought of Amber freezing to death.

She put on a brave show of confidence. "Don't worry, we'll get her back for you." She was shocked by Alex's pale, tear-stained face, her tiny, distressed voice.

"Don't let her die, please!"

"Now Alex, we're all doing our best, love." Jeremy Hastings looked around the room for something to stand on.

She sobbed quietly and hid her face as her dad put a

chair in the middle of the room and began to push at the snow-covered window in the sloping ceiling.

Mandy waited impatiently, hoping that the noise wouldn't frighten the kitten outside.

"No good, it's frozen solid." Mr. Hastings gave up and jumped to the floor.

"What about the other one?" Mandy had seen the shape of a second window.

"In William's room!" He left Alex crying and ran next door, bursting in without knocking.

Mandy followed. What was William making of all this? She saw him on his bed, pale and silent, pretending to read a book, but obviously scared. She stood under the skylight while Mr. Hastings ran for a chair to stand on. Looking down, she saw that the fawn carpet had a darker stain, a patch of wet about ten inches across.

William followed her gaze. He slammed his book shut and glowered.

Had water leaked in through the window frame? Mandy looked up. Or had snow drifted in through the open window? This window was lower, just out of reach. She shot another glance at Alex's brother, who went whiter still. His lip began to quiver as he heard his dad coming back.

"William?" It struck Mandy all at once; that was how

Amber had gotten stuck on the roof. The boy had opened the window and put her there on purpose! Then he'd slammed it shut and locked her out!

"Don't tell!" he whispered, guilty, terrified.

Mr. Hastings dashed in and put the chair over the wet patch without noticing it. He climbed up on it. This time, the window opened easily. He eased it up and propped it into position. "Come on, Mandy, take a look. See if you can coax Amber down from here."

Recovering from her shock, she stood on the chair and peered out. She was closer to Amber but still not

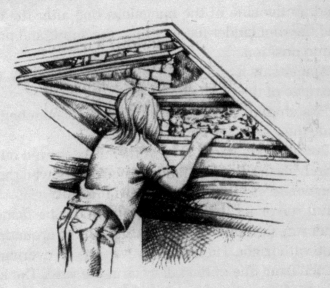

able to reach. The kitten saw her, but this time she didn't react. She blinked and shivered but didn't try to escape.

Mandy knew the signs. This was worse than before; Amber was so cold that she was growing sleepy. But it was the kind of sleep before she fell unconscious and froze to death. "Amber, here!" Mandy cried. She tried desperately to slither onto the roof.

"Careful!" Mr. Hastings yelled.

Out on the road, an SPCA van pulled up at last. From her vantage point, she could see two men rush into the Hastings's yard with special roof ladders. They scrambled up the side of the bungalow, one after the other, laid the roof ladder flat on top of the snow, and pushed it into position.

Amber saw it and gave a cry. She darted away, along the ridge of the roof, almost slipped and fell.

"Watch out!" Mandy warned. The first man began to scale the roof. "She might fall!"

But it was now or never. If the kitten stayed out any longer, she might die. Mandy hoped and prayed that the men would succeed where she had failed.

But terror jerked Amber into action. She made another run, farther out of reach. She looked around, eyes wide with fright. There, just above, was an overhanging branch from one of the tall trees in the yard. The kitten saw it and crouched. The man hesitated. Then he lunged to grab her.

Amber jumped. She sprang up onto the nearest branch. It dipped and swayed. The kitten hung on.

"I've lost her!" the man shouted. Outside, someone else yelled, and the traffic on the road rumbled by. The dark shadow of the tree had swallowed Amber.

"Quick!" Mandy slid back into the bedroom, bringing a shower of loose snow with her. She ran out through the hall onto the porch. Her mom stood with her bag, ready to treat the kitten. "She's up in the tree. We can't see her!"

"Bring a flashlight!" Emily Hope told Jeremy Hastings. They ran to the base of the tree.

"Shine it up into the branches!" The SPCA man held his own flashlight. The yellow beams shone through the dark.

"She's up there somewhere!" Mandy whispered. "She has to be!"

But though the SPCA men brought their ladder and climbed up once more, they couldn't find Amber.

"She can't just disappear!" Frantic, Mandy ran into the road to see if she could see Amber from out there. The moon shone through the bare branches; there was no sign.

"Watch the cars!" Mr. Hastings warned.

Mandy kept close to the side, searching the road just in case the kitten had lost her balance and fallen. Again, nothing!

Amber's mighty leap from rooftop to tree had ended in mystery. They searched and searched, but the kitten seemed to have vanished into thin air!

Six

"What shall I tell Alex?" Mr. Hastings asked as he clicked off his flashlight.

They felt empty and cold. The men from the SPCA had stacked their ladders on top of the van and driven away from Beechtrees.

"I think we should tell her the truth." Mandy's mom offered to help him explain.

They trudged into the house. Mrs. Hastings brought Alex from her room and they broke the news that Amber was lost. There were tearful questions: "How can she be? Isn't she stuck on the roof? Where is she now?"

The grown-ups were gentle, but they had to admit that they had failed.

"At least until it gets light," her mom told her. "Then we can begin to look again. We'll be able to see more in the daylight."

"But it's so cold!" Alex shivered with fear. "Why can't we try to find her *now*?"

"We *have* looked for a long time," Mr. Hastings began. But he saw the look in Alex's green eyes. "OK, I'll try again."

Mandy said she would go with him, while Mrs. Hastings and her mom did their best to calm Alex.

"William, come and give us a hand," Jeremy Hastings called from the front porch.

The boy's bedroom door opened slowly. When he saw Mandy, he closed it quickly again.

"What's gotten into him?" His father was impatient. "As if we didn't have enough to worry about, without William going into a sulk."

Mandy waited while he went to fetch his son. William appeared reluctantly, grumbling about having to go out in the cold. He avoided Mandy's gaze.

"It isn't even my kitten," he complained, as his dad made him put on his jacket and boots.

"But Alex is upset. Don't you want to help us find Amber for her sake?"

William screwed his mouth up tight. He said nothing.

"Come on, try and put someone else first for a change." Mr. Hastings handed them each a flashlight and they went outside. They searched behind bushes along a low wall, across the lawn where the two snowmen still stood, gleaming white in the moonlight.

"Let's look for paw prints," Mandy suggested. She aimed her flashlight at the ground. "If Amber did fall out of the tree and manage to run off, we should soon be able to pick up her trail."

For a while, their search had a new purpose. Surely Mandy was right; the kitten would have left some evidence in the snow. But the minutes ticked by. They looked on the lawn, then under the beech tree for the telltale prints. Mr. Hastings even went up his ladder to investigate the roof for fresh signs. He had no luck up there, either.

"I'm freezing!" William moaned. He sniffled and whined. "My toes hurt! I can't feel my fingers!"

"Well, just think how cold Amber must be!" Mr. Hastings refused to let him retreat into the house. "Now go with Mandy and look on the road. Watch out for cars!"

"It's all clear," Mandy called. She stood at the gate, shining her flashlight along the wall top where the tree branches hung over the road. "Can you see any prints?" she asked William.

He scowled. "No. And it's not my fault if the stupid cat is missing! Why can't Alex take better care of her?"

Mandy bit her tongue. She hated it when people called animals stupid. All of a sudden she had to say something. "Listen, William!" She pulled him to one side and whispered urgently.

"Let go! What?"

"Are you sure it's not your fault that Amber is missing? What about that patch of melted snow on your carpet?"

"Don't blame me. I was only trying to rescue the stupid thing before Mom went and called you!" He looked at her at last, eyes flashing angrily. "Anyway, I know you won't believe me. No one ever does. They never blame Alex. It's always me!" He pulled his sleeve free and ran into the yard. Mandy quickly followed.

She saw William jump the low wall onto the lawn. He headed straight for the snowmen that he and James had built, threw himself at the nearest one, and began shoving and kicking it until it toppled and shattered. It lay in frozen lumps. Soon he had destroyed the second one, too.

"There!" He turned to her, as his father came running down the path. "That's what I think of stupid snowmen. And I hope you never find Amber! I hope she freezes to death!"

* * *

"He didn't really mean it," Dr. Emily explained as she drove Mandy home.

"He sounded as if he did." Mandy had been shocked by the outburst. In the end, Mrs. Hastings had come out and taken William inside.

"He is only seven, remember. And his family has a lot of problems at the moment."

"Yes, and William's making them worse." Mandy couldn't forgive his cruel taunt about Amber. She sat looking out at the snow-covered hillside, staring disaster in the face. For one thing, there were the snags over Father Christmas. Grandma and Grandpa's fundraising treat could well fall completely flat. For another, Alex was so upset about Amber that she might be too ill to enjoy the procession even if it did take place. And then, of course, there was the kitten out all night in the cold.

"I'm sure he doesn't mean to make things worse," her mom insisted. "I don't think he can help it, poor boy." She swung down their lane, talking things through. "It must be hard for him, having a little sister who gets all the attention. Alex is ill, so naturally her mom and dad worry about her. They don't have much time to spare for William at the moment. I expect he feels left out."

"Jealous?" Mandy considered it for the first time.

"But that doesn't mean he had to go and spoil the snowmen. That makes no sense."

"Sometimes things don't make sense." They turned into their own drive and pulled up in the yard.

"Mom . . . ?" Frowning, Mandy unclicked her seat belt. "I know what you mean. William's getting his own back."

"Yes. But he's having to take it out on things that never did anything to him in the first place. Like the snowmen."

"And Amber?" Mandy wondered out loud. William had denied it, but the suspicion lingered that he was the one who had put the kitten on the roof.

"Possibly." Dr. Emily listened quietly to the full story as Mandy saw it. She sighed. "Oh, dear, I hope not. The poor boy must be feeling wretched."

"Poor *Alex*, poor *Amber*!" If it was true, William had taken out his problem on the thing his sister loved best. And now an innocent animal was suffering because of it.

"Cheer up!" Adam Hope greeted them with a smile. "Don't tell me you didn't see them out in the yard?"

Mandy shook her head wearily. "No. Who?"

"Not who; what. The van and trailer. Don's back!"

"Och aye, I'm back, all right." The wiry Scotsman

came downstairs in T-shirt, jeans, and bare feet. "I've had a long, hot bath and now I'm ready to put my feet up in front of the TV."

"Is Dasher with you?" It took a while to sink in. The last Mandy had heard was that the trailer was stuck in a snowdrift outside a Leeds hospital.

"Aye, and young James. All home safe and sound." Don's face was shiny red after his bath. "Now where did I put those sneakers?" He scratched his head and began to search the kitchen.

"But how did you get here?" For a moment Mandy had a vision of the reindeer rising magically above the rooftops, pulling the sleigh.

"The snowplows dug us out. They did a great job. By late afternoon they had the traffic moving again. We couldn't get a message through to you, so we headed for home. It's a good wee story, though." He chuckled over it. "Now where *did* I put those shoes?"

"At least I won't have to get dressed up in that red suit." Dr. Adam sounded relieved. He made Mandy sit down to her supper. "You had us worried for a while, Don. Mandy's grandpa has been all over the village trying to round up a substitute."

"And no one wanted to do it," Mandy added. She ate her supper, glad that at least one of the major crises was over. "Everyone said, 'Let me think about it,' which means, 'No,' doesn't it? But anyway, Rudolph's better and you're back."

"No problem!" Don was cheery as ever. "Maybe I left them in my bag," he muttered to himself. He shuffled off in bare feet, upstairs to the spare room. They heard a few thumps and clomps as he came back down — shoes on but unlaced, and wearing a puzzled frown. "That's not like me. I'm usually a very organized sort of person!"

Mandy rolled her eyes at her mom and dad. Don was

many good things, but organized wasn't one of them. "What have you lost?"

"Och, I wouldn't say 'lost' exactly. More mislaid. Aye, but I could have sworn I put them in my bag."

"Your shoes? They're on your feet, Don." Mandy broke it to him gently.

"Och, no, not my shoes. No, I'm talking about Father Christmas's clothes; the old gentleman's best red suit and black boots. I told him I'd spruce them up for Christmas Eve, so he left them with me. I've looked, and I can't find them anywhere!"

"He left them at the hospital," Adam Hope confirmed as he came in to say good night to Mandy. "They just called and left a message. Father Christmas's suit is neatly folded on a bed in an empty side ward!"

Mandy made a noise halfway between a groan and a giggle.

"Yes, and you thought *I* was absent-minded!" He sat down for a moment on the edge of her bed. "Your mom says you've had a hard day?"

She nodded. "We looked everywhere for Amber, Dad, but we just couldn't find her. What do you think could have happened to her?" She knew that she was so worried she wouldn't sleep.

Her dad shrugged. "I don't know for sure, but let's try

and work it out. Because one thing's for sure; a cat really can't just vanish. So, first off, you say she definitely jumped off the roof?"

"Yes, into the tree by the wall. We saw her land, but it was so dark among the branches that we lost sight of her."

"And she's absolutely, definitely not still up there?"

"No. So where can she be?"

"Well . . ." He spoke gently. "We have to face the fact that Amber might have fallen."

Mandy scrunched up her face and closed her eyes. She didn't want to hear this.

"No, listen, love. Say she did fall; after all, it was dark and she was very frightened. But you know cats have this amazing ability to land on their feet. We call it a head-on-body righting reflex."

She opened her eyes to look at him. "Meaning what?"

"It works like this. A cat falls from a height. First it twists so that the top of its head faces upward. Then the neck and body line up in the reflex action so that the cat falls feet first. It only takes milliseconds, and lo and behold, she lands safely. One of her nine lives is saved!"

Mandy took a deep breath. "Do you think that's what happened to Amber?"

"It's possible. She falls and lands the right way up, no

damage done. Then as quick as she can she darts for cover, waits for all the fuss to die down."

"Yes. Maybe she didn't like the flashlights and all the noise." Mandy pictured the kitten tucked safely out of harm's way, sheltered from the wind and waiting for the all clear. Tomorrow morning the Hastings would open their front door and discover her, sitting on the mat and meowing for her breakfast. "I just hope she found a nice warm place to hide."

"Me, too." Her dad stood up and turned off the light. "After a day like today, we deserve some luck. So try not to worry too much, OK?"

The door closed and left the room in darkness. Mandy tried to sleep. But one thing bothered her. If her dad was right, and Amber had landed safely, why hadn't they found any paw prints in the snow? Mandy wrestled with the problem until well after midnight. No paw prints, no evidence, nothing. Poor little Amber; it seemed that she had simply been spirited away.

Seven

Grandma turned up at Animal Ark before breakfast, armed with scissors, sewing pins, and an armful of old red curtain material. "We'll just have to make do and mend!" she cried, seizing hold of Don. She measured him for a replacement Father Christmas suit. "I expect Santa Claus is about the same size as you," she said with a wink.

"Aye, though he's a wee bit fatter around the waist." Don patted his stomach.

As usual, Mandy played along. She helped Grandma get him ready for the grand procession that evening.

They laid the fabric flat on the kitchen table, cut and shaped it, then Grandma began to sew to the whirr of the machine, making tucks, seams, and fastenings. By nine o'clock, Don was trying on the finished article.

"Beard?" Grandma stood back to judge the effect.

"Cotton balls!" Mandy ran into the clinic. She dived through the busy waiting room, grabbed a pack from a cabinet, and raced back to the house. By hook or by crook they would be ready for the big event.

"Boots?" Grandma was almost finished. The beard was a miracle of cardboard, glue, and cotton balls, with elastic loops to hook over the ears.

"Dad's rain boots!" Mandy jumped up to get them. Then, when they were satisfied and Don had gone outside to groom Rudolph and Dasher so that they would look their best for that evening, she called James to see if he would come along to Beechtrees with her.

"What time is it? Have you called them yet?" James inquired sleepily.

"No, not yet." Mandy had been putting it off. "And they haven't called us, either." Her hopes that Amber would turn up on the doorstep of the bungalow were fading. She knew that the Hastings would have telephoned with any good news about the kitten. "I wondered if you would come and help us look." She would be glad if he said yes. James was wonderful in a crisis. He kept a clear head and always came up with bright ideas.

"Sure. What time?"

"In half an hour."

"See you there." He was alert now and didn't waste time talking.

In fact, he was at the bungalow before her. When Mandy arrived, he was already looking for the lost kitten with Mrs. Hastings. Mr. Hastings had gone to work at the tennis club, and William and Alex were inside.

"How is she?" Mandy asked.

"Not quite so upset as yesterday. But she's very sad," Mrs. Hastings told them. "I can't think of anything to cheer her up. She's completely lost interest in Christmas."

Mandy knew how Alex must feel. Even making Father Christmas's outfit with Grandma hadn't stopped her from worrying about Amber. "Should I go in and see her?"

"Would you mind, Mandy? You're the only person Alex is interested in talking to right now. I'm afraid she sees you as some kind of heroine, like Superwoman!" Mrs. Hastings gave a sad smile and led Mandy and James through the hallway.

James stayed in the kitchen while Mandy tiptoed into Alex's quiet room. The curtains were drawn, and a dim lamp shone. All around the walls, pictures of animals seemed to stare down at the sick little girl who lay motionless in bed.

"Hi, Alex." Mandy sat close by. There was a full glass of water on the bedside table, next to an unopened book.

Alex turned her head. When she spoke, her voice was a whisper. "Hello, Mandy. Guess what, I don't think Father Christmas read my letter."

"Why not?" Mandy saw now what Mr. and Mrs. Hastings meant when they insisted that Alex must keep calm. Being upset drained her of her strength. She looked as white as a ghost.

"I wrote and asked him for a collar for Amber; one with a little bell."

"Well, you never know." She tried to sound cheerful. "He might bring you one. He hasn't delivered his presents yet, remember!"

Alex's eyes filled with tears. "No, but if he got my note, he'd know I have a kitten. Then he wouldn't let Amber get lost, would he?"

"I don't think even Father Christmas can do anything about a missing kitten," Mandy explained gently.

"But he knows everything! He knows what we'd all like for Christmas. He can even fly through the air with his reindeer. He must know about Amber!"

Mandy nodded. "Well, maybe he does."

Alex had a sudden idea. She wiped her eyes and looked at Mandy. "Yes, and maybe he's looking after her for me! That could be where Amber is right now — with Father Christmas!"

"I hope so," Mandy whispered. Before Mrs. Hastings came in to give Alex her medicine, Mandy crept out of the room to join James in the kitchen.

After a few minutes Mrs. Hastings followed. "She's sleeping," she reported. "It's an extra strain on her heart when she's upset. She isn't strong enough to take it." It was Alex's mother's turn to brush away a tear.

"Come on, let's start," James suggested, ready to take up the search. They went out onto the porch.

"I dread what sort of time we'll have if we don't find this kitten." Mrs. Hastings scanned the trampled lawn. "We've been over and over the ground, but there's still no sign."

James agreed. "I thought we might find prints in the snow, but it's all trodden down, so even if there was a track last night, it's disappeared by now."

"I did look," Mandy told him. "And I couldn't see one. William and I even searched out on the road." She glanced at the house to see the small, pale face and ginger hair of Alex's brother staring solemnly at them through the window.

James studied the beech tree where Amber had last

been seen. Then he went out to look at the road, which was quiet at this time of day. He stood under the over-hanging branches and looked up, pushing his hair from his forehead. "Who saw her up there?"

"Let's think; me, Mom, Mr. Hastings, and the two men from the SPCA."

"And the people driving by," James suggested. "If Amber managed to scramble down the tree on this side, then ran off, maybe someone in a car saw her?"

Mandy nodded. "All we need is one clue to find out which way she went. But how do we find out if anybody saw her?"

"We could ask in the village. There would be plenty of people around on Christmas Eve, doing their last-minute shopping. It's worth a try!"

Mrs. Hastings agreed. "You two go and ask. I'll stay here and make some fliers to put up on trees and gateposts to say we've lost a kitten. I'll get Alex and William to help me." She seemed glad to have some-thing to do.

So Mandy and James went into Welford. They called at the McFarlanes' and the Fox and Goose. They saw James's dad talking in the square to Mrs. Collins. They saw Ernie Bell and Walter Pickard.

"Tom's right as rain!" Walter called. "Back to normal, as bossy as ever!"

They passed the message; the Hastings's kitten, Amber, was lost in the snow. Had anyone seen a stray tortoiseshell with bright golden eyes? Each time the answer came back: "No, sorry. But we will keep a lookout!" Even the people who remembered driving past the bungalow at about the right time hadn't seen a thing.

They asked the Parker Smythes and Sam Western, as well as the farmer from Graystones, David Gill. All promised to do their best, but they shook their heads as if to say, "What chance does a little kitten have out in the freezing cold at this time of year?"

By lunchtime Mandy and James had done all they could. They headed back past the square, where Julian Hardy from the pub was stringing up big Christmas lights. "Ready for Father Christmas," he said. "I hear everything's going ahead?"

Mandy nodded. Her legs were weary from tramping through the snow. And so far, all for nothing. They were no nearer to finding Amber. She forgot to mention to Mr. Hardy that Don McNab and Dasher were back in Welford, ready for tonight's procession.

"We're busy baking mince pies. And John's made Christmas candles for the kids. The vicar's bringing a tape of Christmas carols, and I'll rig up loudspeakers so we can all sing along."

Everyone was pulling out all the stops in support of

Alex's lifesaving trip to America. Mandy and James watched for a while, then went on, deep in thought. "You know something?" Mandy said, "Unless we find Amber, I don't think Alex will go!"

"For her operation?" James began to see how important the missing kitten was. "You mean, she's just too upset?"

Mandy sighed and nodded. "And too ill to travel. Come on, we'd better go and see what's happening."

"If only *I'd* seen something." James strode along beside her. "Don and I drove along this road yesterday afternoon, on our way back from Leeds."

"Along with a hundred other cars." She was beginning to feel that it was like looking for a needle in a haystack.

"Well, it looks like William is finally trying to help." James spotted him in the garden. William climbed the wall and stood, watching them approach. As they drew near, he dropped to the ground and ran to meet them.

"Alex is even more sick! They went and got the doctor." His eyes were wide and scared. "Did you find the kitten?"

Looking up the drive, they saw a red car and the front door of the bungalow standing open. A tall woman came out carrying a dark bag. She stopped to talk earnestly to Mrs. Hastings. The moment William spotted them, he ducked behind the wall. "That's her," he told them. "That's the doctor!"

They waited until the woman had gotten into her car, backed out of the drive, and driven off. By this time, William was shaking from head to foot.

"I never meant for her to get sick!" He trembled and fought back the tears, refusing to go any nearer to his house. The front door was closed, the bungalow strangely quiet.

"Just like you never meant Amber to get lost in the snow?" Mandy asked quietly.

James stepped back in surprise. William hung his head. "I only wanted her to be on the roof for a little while. I didn't know she wouldn't come down again." He mumbled and choked over how his plan had gone wrong.

"You mean, *you* put Amber up there?" James was stunned.

Mandy nodded. "I thought so. Listen." She knew the whole story would soon come tumbling out.

"Yes, but I thought I could get her down again. They'd all be looking for her, and I'd be the one who saved her, see?"

"But it didn't work out," said Mandy. Instead of rescuing the kitten and being the hero, William had to watch Amber climb out of reach on the roof, then get too scared to move, slowly growing colder and colder as night fell. "Why didn't you tell someone?"

"I was scared," he confessed. "I thought Amber was going to die because of me." Tears welled up and rolled down his cheeks.

"Look, don't worry about that now." James knew there was no point crying over it. "At least we know how it happened."

Mandy wondered how James could be so kind. She found it hard to forgive William. But the little boy looked

miserable as he realized just what he'd done, and Mandy remembered what her mom had said; William was feeling left out. He was a lonely child who knew he'd done something wrong. "We won't tell anyone," she whispered. "Don't cry any more. Just help us find Amber!"

William sniffed and dried his eyes on his cuff. "I don't want to go in," he pleaded.

"OK." James was practical. "Let's stay outside and look."

"Again!" Mandy stood at the gates, hands on her hips. It almost drove her crazy to think how often they'd gone over this ground since Amber had disappeared.

But William shook his head. "No!" he insisted. He pulled back as James tried to persuade him to come into the yard.

"Why not? The least you can do is help us look!" For the first time, James sounded angry.

"I can't. Anyway, there isn't any point!"

Mandy turned. "Don't, James. What's wrong, William?" She suspected there was more to come.

"Amber's not here."

"How do you know? Did you see what happened?"

Slowly he nodded. "I was looking out of the window. She was in the tree. Everyone was using ladders and flashlights, but I knew there wasn't any point."

"Why not? What did you see?" She wanted to shake the truth out of him, but she forced herself to be patient.

William stood at the roadside, pointing up at the tree. "She was in that branch, there. I saw her. I shouted, but you didn't hear because there was too much noise." There was a long pause. "Amber fell."

"Where? Into the road?" James was the one to prompt him, as Mandy held her breath.

"No. She fell onto a sort of truck. I saw her slip from the branch. The next second the truck went past the gate and I saw Amber on top of it, hanging on."

"Alive?" Mandy gasped.

He nodded. "The truck kept going. I couldn't stop it."

James's mind flew ahead. Mandy was dazed but overjoyed that Amber had survived the fall. "What kind of truck?" he asked.

"A gray one. It was a kind of trailer."

James stared. "What was pulling the trailer?"

Mandy grabbed James's arm, waiting in suspense for the reply.

"A big van, a dirty white one. It was covered in snow. I've never seen it before."

They gasped. "Don!" they said together.

"The reindeer's trailer!" Now, at this moment, Mandy

could have hugged William. Here was the clue they needed. "Amber fell on top of it!"

"It looks like it," James breathed. "The kitten must have driven home with Don and me!"

"To Animal Ark!" Mandy cried. "Oh, James, Alex was right; Father Christmas has been looking after Amber all along!"

Eight

"William saw what happened to Amber!" Mandy told Mrs. Hastings, so excited that she could hardly get the words out. "At last we've picked up a lead we can follow!"

Mrs. Hastings went right away to tell Alex the latest news while William slipped quietly back into the house. "I won't get her hopes up too high just yet," Alex's mom said. "But at least this should help to cheer her up!"

"We hope!" James whispered to Mandy as they set off down the road, as fast as they could, toward Animal Ark. Back at Animal Ark, Mandy and James found the reindeer's trailer standing in the yard. Its doors hung open and the ramp was down. They nearly fell over themselves getting inside it. Their feet thumped up the ramp, and they almost tumbled over.

But, once inside, they soon realized that the dark trailer was empty. Mandy had longed for it to be simple. She had hoped Amber had clung onto the top of the trailer and during the journey home had clambered inside to safety — to spend the night in the warm straw. But no, the trailer was bare. No kitten, not even any straw.

"Don must have cleaned it out," James said, his voice flat.

"Let's make sure." Mandy took one last look around, then went out and hoisted herself up onto a ledge to look on top. There was no kitten there, but something caught her eyes. "James, come and look at this!"

James joined her. Together they peered onto the snowy roof of the trailer.

"See there." She pointed.

Frozen into the deep snow was a trail of paw prints that led from a scuffed patch. "You think that's where Amber fell?"

"Yes, then she crept to that far edge, there."

"Well, at least we know William's telling the truth,"

James agreed. "But that's not to say that Amber stayed there all the way back here." He jumped down and tried to think what to do next.

"Let's ask Don if he knows anything." Mandy caught sight of him in the compound with the two reindeer. "Don!"

He waved as she ran over.

"Don, did you just muck out the trailer?"

"I did." He hummed cheerfully. Rudolph was enjoying a grooming session, getting ready for the big night. Dasher nibbled at a dish of sugar beets.

"Did you see anything there?" Again she was in such a rush that the words tumbled out. "Like a kitten, for instance?"

"Whoa, slow down!" His eyes crinkled with amusement. Mandy hopped from foot to foot, and now James came running. Rudolph grunted and nudged at Don's hand. "Aye, steady on, Rudi. I haven't forgotten you!"

"A brown-and-black tortoiseshell kitten with amber eyes!" Mandy gave a full description to a mystified Don.

"Aye, as it happens, I did."

"Oh!" Mandy clasped her hands together. "Oh, Don, where is she? What did you do with her?"

"Well, I didn't do anything with her." He scratched his

head. "I went into the box and there she was, curled up in the straw, cozy as you like. Cheeky wee thing."

"You didn't chase her away?" James asked anxiously.

"Och, what do you take me for? It was a pity to disturb her; she'd found a grand spot for a wee nap. No, I went off to fetch her a saucer of milk, but wouldn't you just know it? The minute I turned my back, off she ran." He shrugged and started again on Rudolph's thick coat. "She's a wicked wee cat, right enough."

Mandy stared. "She ran off?" she faltered.

"Aye, but don't worry. Kittens don't stray far from home. You'll soon have her back safe and sound."

"No," James cut in. "Amber doesn't belong to Mandy. She doesn't live here at Animal Ark."

"But I thought you said you were looking for her?" Don stood up straight and wrinkled his forehead.

"For someone else," James explained. "Did you see which way she ran?" Of course, Don couldn't realize how important this was. They'd been so near to finding Amber, yet now they'd lost her again.

He sighed. "I didn't. She nipped away when my back was turned. I just got on and mucked out as usual. I never gave the wee cat a second thought."

Mandy hid her disappointment. "Never mind. Thanks, Don."

"Och, I've a feeling I've let you down," he apologized.

"No." She managed to smile. "At least we know Amber was here."

"How long ago?" James fitted together all the information he could gather.

"Half an hour. Maybe a wee bit longer."

Mandy nodded at James. "Then she can't have gone far!" she said, jutting out her chin and looking across the yard. The hunt for Amber was on.

In the small village of Welford, news of the missing kitten traveled fast.

"Little Alex Hastings is ill with worry, poor child!" Mrs. Ponsonby spread the word. She'd heard it from Emily Hope when she went into the clinic with snuffly Pandora. She told Mrs. McFarlane that the kitten was still alive. "Isn't that wonderful? And wouldn't it be the best Christmas present in the world if we all helped to find her?" Warmhearted in spite of her bossy manner, Mrs. Ponsonby gathered a search party.

"I suppose I've nothing better to do." Ernie Bell hid his willingness to help beneath a grumpy surface. He picked up a shovel from his garden shed and set off for Animal Ark, ready to dig through snowdrifts and do his very best.

Walter Pickard, not to be outdone, went with him. "We can't have the little lass making herself sick over it, can we?"

And John Hardy, the serious, studious son of the landlord, went along with Susan Collins. Even Brandon Gill, the shy boy from Graystones Farm, heard about Amber and tramped across the snowy fields to Mandy's house. Soon a dozen people, young and old, were helping James and Mandy in the search for Amber.

"We must spread out in different directions!" Mrs. Ponsonby was wearing a bright pink anorak with a white fake-fur trim. She had a master plan. "Mandy and James have checked the house thoroughly, so we can be sure that the kitten has gone farther afield. We will split into twos and search the lane with a fine-tooth comb. Now, Mandy, please give a detailed description." She clapped her hands quickly. "Attention everyone, please!"

Mandy blushed as she gave the information. "Amber is a black-and-brown tortoiseshell with golden-orange eyes. Her tail is mostly black. There's a flash of white on one back leg. She's five months old." Even as she spoke, she realized that the short daylight hours would soon draw to a close. They must get the search underway as soon as possible.

They left it to Mrs. Ponsonby to divide people into

pairs. "Walter, you come along with me!" she instructed, after she'd sent all the others off.

Mandy raised her eyebrows. James breathed a sigh of relief. Walter got no chance to object.

"Go on, Mandy. You and James head for Lilac Cottage. See if your grandparents have seen or heard anything useful!" Mrs. Ponsonby implied that the two of them were slacking.

They shot off, leaving Walter to be bossed around by her, passing Brandon and Susan who had been sent to look in the field opposite Animal Ark.

"Here!" Susan said, suddenly excited. She pointed to a track that led right across the field. "A set of footprints!"

James and Mandy jumped the ditch to peer over the wall.

Brandon stopped to examine them. "A fox," he said quietly, shaking his head.

"Oh, Brandon, are you sure?" Susan was dismayed. She clung onto her discovery. "But they look like cat prints to me!"

"Fox," he said stubbornly. "They're too heavy for a kitten."

Susan sighed and gave in. Mandy and James jumped back into the lane and went on. The snow still lay deep and pretty as a Christmas card along all the wall tops and gates, weighing down the dark tree branches. By the time they reached the cottage, they'd passed Ernie, John Hardy, and Mr. Hastings, who'd rushed over from work the moment he heard the news.

"Thanks, you two!" He raised his head and called after him. "You don't know how much we appreciate this!"

"Thank us later," Mandy told him.

"When we find Amber!" James added.

At Lilac Cottage, Grandpa stood holding the gate open for them. "Come on. Your grandmother and I have been having a good look around, but no luck so far, I'm afraid."

It was the same old story; everyone doing their best but getting nowhere.

"That kitten certainly has a knack for vanishing!" Grandma was in the front garden, looking under benches and behind bare trellises where, in the summer, roses grew.

"Poor thing. It must be a big, cold world out there for her." Grandpa pictured her lost and frightened. It made James and Mandy concentrate even harder.

"Here, Mandy!" James called at last. His warm breath turned to clouds of steam as he trod carefully in Mr. Hope's vegetable garden at the back of the cottage. "Come and look!"

Mandy walked delicately between the mysterious white humps and clumps. Under the snow lay Grandpa's precious rhubarb and fruit bushes. Her footsteps were the first to spoil the smooth surface of the carefully tended ground.

James crouched by a round water barrel at the bottom of the garden. The barrel was covered over with a thick layer of ice, but it was the base that he was interested in. There, around the back of the barrel, leading along the garden boundary toward the house, was a beautiful, clear set of paw prints!

"What do you think?" he breathed. "Not a fox's this time?"

"Definitely not! Not so close to the house." She followed the track to see where it led. "Anyway, they're too small for a fox."

Excited now, they followed the trail onto the patio. They lost it, then found it again. The prints led along the patio, straight up to the sliding glass doors.

Mandy turned to James. "What now?"

He shook his head. "It looks like she went inside."

"But who would let her in? Grandma and Grandpa would have mentioned it." Doubts came to the surface; doubts that she didn't want to admit.

James pressed his face to the glass and peered inside. "Uh, Mandy . . ." he said dully.

She forced herself to look. *Please let it be Amber!* she prayed. But there, sitting peacefully in his favorite armchair, carefully grooming behind his ears, was the sleek gray shape of Smoky, Grandma and Grandpa's own precious cat.

Nine

Smoky saw two surprised faces peering in at him. He opened his mouth in a great big yawn. Then he stood and arched his back, rousing himself from sleep.

For the first time ever, Mandy wasn't glad to see him. In fact, her heart gave a thud of disappointment. As Smoky leaped from his chair and came padding across the carpet toward them, tail up, ready to say hello, she turned away.

"No, wait a minute . . ." James chewed his lip. "Maybe Smoky can help us!"

Mandy didn't see how. She stood on the patio, trying to get over this latest disappointment. Grandpa's garden, all covered with snow, with its bare apple trees and empty greenhouse, looked as bleak as she felt. Would they ever find Amber?

"Mandy, listen!" James insisted. "This garden is Smoky's territory. He thinks it belongs to him."

She agreed. "That's right. He keeps watch over it."

"Just like Eric at home. He has a track that he follows, like the one by the fence. He kind of travels a network of paths on his home turf." He knew that male cats were especially anxious to keep invaders out.

Mandy began to see what he was getting at. "So, if there's another cat around, Smoky would soon chase him off."

"Or *her*!" James suggested. He stared through the glass door at Smoky, who meowed silently to be let out.

"You mean, if Amber is anywhere around here, Smoky would soon find out?"

James nodded. His eyes were wide with excitement behind his round glasses. "What do you think?"

"It's worth a try!" Immediately Mandy seized the handle and slid the door open for Smoky to step out. "Come on, Smoky. There's a good cat." She stopped to stroke him and let him rub against her leg. He trod delicately into the snow, lifted one front paw, and shook it.

James eased the door closed behind him. "Just in case he prefers to run back inside into the warmth!" he whispered.

Smoky raised his head and looked around at the strange white world. His ears twitched and he followed the flight of a sparrow from Grandpa's fence to the apple tree. He flicked his tail and meowed.

Mandy and James held their breath. They watched Smoky stalk toward the tree. He crouched by the gnarled trunk, staring up at the sparrow. The bird hopped and twittered in the branches above. As Smoky sprang for the trunk and his claws dug into the bark, the sparrow fluttered and flew off. Smoky dropped silently to the ground, disappointed.

When cats chased birds, they were like tigers, Mandy thought. Or like jaguars stalking through the jungle. Smoky settled low on the ground, haunches raised, tail flicking to and fro.

"What's he seen now?" James breathed. They didn't dare move as Smoky marked out his territory and went prowling through the garden between the rows of snow-covered vegetables.

"Shh!" Mandy crept quietly after the cat. Smoky had picked up a scent. He padded around the water barrel, set off on his track by the fence, sniffed again, then turned back in his tracks. He trotted quickly toward the greenhouse, stopped by a half-buried stack of over-turned flowerpots, and hissed.

They heard a tiny noise, a faint, frightened meow. The fur rose along Smoky's back as he arched and let out a loud yowl. Mandy and James ran for the greenhouse as fast as their legs would carry them.

Yet, when they got there, expecting to find Amber cowering in a corner, there was only Smoky. He hissed and growled, the fur on his back standing on end as he arched and spat.

"Let's look inside the greenhouse!" Mandy dived for the door. She wrenched it open and peered inside. Empty shelves, empty flowerpots and trays. No kitten.

"Out here!" James listened again and traced the fee-ble meow to the row of overturned pots. Some had top-pled sideways and lay higgledy-piggledy around the back of the greenhouse. They were heavy clay pots, big enough for a kitten to get trapped inside. . . .

Mandy rushed to help. The faint pleas grew louder. Smoky backed off. He sensed danger and crept to the edge of the vegetable patch, where he crouched, growl-ing steadily.

"She must be stuck under one of these pots!" James tried to reach down the narrow gap between the green-house and a tall fence. He overbalanced and fell against the glass panes. The whole greenhouse shook, but nothing broke. Instead, there was the sliding, rushing sound of heavy snow gliding down a smooth slope.

Mandy glanced up at the greenhouse roof. An avalanche of snow hung over the edge, a huge weight of snow just above James's head. "Watch out!" She darted to pull him clear.

Just in time! The snow inched down the roof, hung for a second, then plunged to the ground in a shuddering thud. The kitten's cries were drowned as a mountain of snow buried her alive.

Grandma and Grandpa Hope came rushing from the front of the house. "What was that?" Grandpa had heard the noise. He stared in dismay at the solid mass of snow.

"Oh, quick!" Mandy cried. "Amber is under there! We heard her, then the snow fell on top of her. We need something to dig her out!"

In a flash Grandpa headed for his garden shed. Grandma rushed into the house to fetch the fireplace shovel. Meanwhile, Mandy and James kneeled to scrape at the pile of snow. There was no sign of Smoky; he had fled across the garden in the rumble of falling snow.

Mandy dug with her bare hands. "What if she's been crushed?" The snow was heavy, packed into the gap between the fence and the greenhouse. It was about three feet deep.

"Don't think about it!" James scrabbled through the heap.

Soon Grandpa came back with his spade. "Try this!" He handed it to Mandy over James's head. She began to dig.

"Careful!" Grandma warned. She gave the smaller shovel to James. He worked at the bottom of the pile, going in sideways.

At last Mandy's spade hit something solid. She scraped at the snow to reveal a cracked flowerpot, tumbled side-

ways under the avalanche. Digging carefully around it, she pulled it free.

"What's under there?" Grandpa craned to see.

"More pots." Mandy put the spade down and began to scoop with her hands again, while James dug his tunnel through the base of the pile.

"We've got to get air in there!" he gasped, his face red with the effort. "Amber has to breathe!"

"Perhaps she's trapped under a pot, in a pocket of air," Grandma whispered.

"I hope you're right," Grandpa murmured.

Mandy pulled a second pot from the heap. It was broken in two. She thought she heard a faint cry from deep in the snow. Her heart leaped. "Did you hear that?" In a frenzy she scraped at the snow, digging deeper and deeper.

"Yes!" James stopped tunneling to listen. "I heard it!"

"Oh, be careful, Mandy!" Grandma repeated. Any second the pile of snow could collapse and crush the kitten to death.

Mandy lifted out another shard of broken pot. The snow shifted and slid. She stopped, gathered her nerve, and began again. This time she brought out a whole flowerpot, then another.

The cries grew louder, more insistent: *Meow . . . meow . . . meow!*

Mandy scraped at the snow. She uncovered a pot. It was turned upside down, like part of a giant sandcastle made of snow. She did more careful scraping. The pot tilted then jolted back into position. The kitten wailed, then went quiet again.

"Ready?" Mandy breathed. She seized the pot with both hands, fingers frozen, arms trembling. She lifted it inch by inch so that the surrounding snow stayed in place. And there, under the flowerpot, hunched in a bedraggled ball, her orange eyes staring up at them, was Amber!

The news spread down the lane like wildfire; Mandy and James had found the kitten. Ernie, Brandon, Susan, and Mr. Hastings came running to Lilac Cottage. Mrs. Ponsonby went to the village to proclaim the good tidings. Walter stopped by Animal Ark to tell the Hopes. Soon everyone knew.

By this time Mandy had carried Amber into the house. She asked her grandmother for a towel and began to rub the kitten dry. Amber shivered and huddled inside the towel, mewing quietly.

"What about a hot water bottle?" Grandpa asked. They were still worried about hypothermia.

"No, she shouldn't have direct heat," Mandy said. "We mustn't warm her up too quickly. We just have to get her dry." She said she didn't think there were any broken bones, but that Amber might have frostbite. She couldn't tell yet.

"Can she have warm milk?" Grandma asked. They stood peering over James's head at Mandy kneeling on the kitchen floor with the kitten on her lap.

Mandy nodded. Soon Amber's fur was dry and fluffy. Grandma brought a saucer of milk and Mandy set her gently on her feet. The kitten wobbled, then stooped to lap with her pink tongue. Mandy rested on her heels and looked up at the worried faces. Her wet blonde hair was streaked across her cheeks and neck. Her skin still tingled with cold. "I think she's going to be all right!" she whispered.

A crowd had gathered outside the gate as Mandy wrapped Amber in a thick red blanket and took her out to Grandpa's camper. They planned to drive to Beechtrees to deliver the kitten safely back home.

"Well done!"

"Isn't that great!"

"Oh, she's gorgeous!" There was a general murmur of approval at the sight of the rescued kitten.

Mandy let the helpers have a peep. There Amber sat, warmly wrapped up, purring like a little engine. She peered out from the red blanket at the row of strange faces, gave a puzzled meow, and snuggled deeper into Mandy's arms.

Grandpa thanked everyone as he opened the gate. "All's well that ends well!" He smiled and went to wait in the van.

Grandma beckoned from the doorstep. "Come on, Mandy. Don't keep that poor little girl waiting a moment longer!" She went to wave them off through the gate.

Mandy sat in the front with Amber, James in the back. Mr. Hastings climbed in too, then slid the door of the camper shut.

They were on their way at last to give Amber back to Alex.

"Just in time," Jeremy Hastings murmured. He stared out the window across the valley at the twinkling lights of Welford village.

Just in time for Christmas, just in time for the grand procession; above all, just in time for Alex.

Mandy took Amber into Alex's bedroom. The kitten was still wrapped in the red woolen blanket. "Look who I've brought," she whispered.

Alex was still in bed, staring at the ceiling. Her hair shone coppery-red against the white pillows. She turned her head, hardly daring to believe her eyes.

Mandy tiptoed forward. "It's Amber!"

"Really and truly?" Alex propped herself on her elbows. Then she sat up. "Let me see!"

She unwrapped the blanket. Amber's round face peered out, eyes alert as she recognized the room. She sprang from Mandy's arms onto the bed and went padding softly toward Alex.

The little girl held her arms wide open. She was speechless with delight. Amber stole straight into her arms. Alex wrapped them around the kitten, put her cheek against Amber's soft head, and looked up at Mandy. "Did Father Christmas tell you where to look?"

Mandy smiled. Alex's dream had come true. No more worries, no more tears. Now she could concentrate on getting better. "In a way, yes, I suppose he did," she said.

Ten

Don McNab was polite about Grandma's specially made Father Christmas outfit. "It's very good of you to go to all this trouble," he said as she brought it into the yard at Animal Ark. He was busy transforming the trailer into the reindeer sleigh. "But the old gentleman won't be needing it after all!"

Mandy and James were helping Don. It was seven o'clock; they had just half an hour to get the sleigh ready and to harness Rudolph and Dasher, before they were due in the village square. The evening was crisp and clear, a perfect Christmas Eve.

"Are you sure?" Grandma was puzzled. As far as she

knew, Don had left the proper outfit stranded in a hospital ward.

"Quite sure, thank you. I got a message to Father Christmas and he had a spare one especially sent down from Reindeerland!"

"Ah, well." She raised her eyebrows, then tucked the homemade suit back into her shopping bag. "Perhaps it will be useful another year." Intrigued by the sleigh, she walked around it. She admired the fiberglass side panels as James bolted them into place and inspected the bulky pile of presents in the back. "Lovely!" she told Mandy. "I may be an old lady, but I confess I'm very excited!"

Mandy nodded. "I know. I can hardly wait."

"They're ready for you in the square," Grandma told Don. "The holiday lights look beautiful. They've hung huge, old-fashioned lanterns outside the pub. And the music is already playing."

"Is there anyone there yet?" Mandy asked. All they needed now for the procession to be a success was a huge crowd of people singing carols, all gathered to see Father Christmas and his sleigh.

"Quite a few. Your grandpa and I are on our way back there now. Would you like a lift?"

But Mandy and James weren't quite ready. "No, thanks. We'll come down with Mom. Dad had to go out on a call, so we'll meet him there." She wanted to help Don hitch Rudolph and Dasher to the sleigh before they set off for the village.

So Grandma said she would see them later. "Don't be too long," she warned, "or you'll miss all the fun!"

But Mandy and James couldn't think of anything better than helping with the reindeer. They went to lead them out of the compound, smartly groomed, hooves clicking, white manes fluffed out. Their velvety antlers cast wonderful shadows across the yard.

"That's right, steady on!" Don encouraged as they entered them in between the shafts of the sleigh. "Come on now, Dasher, back a wee bit farther! That's it, Rudolph, you show him how it's done!" Slowly they eased the reindeer into position.

Dasher grunted and pawed the ground. The sleigh shifted behind him. Rudolph stood, the picture of patience, as if he sensed that their big moment had come.

"Grand!" Don was satisfied at last.

They stood back for the full effect. It was as good as they could possibly imagine; a gleaming sleigh with polished white sides, decorated in red and gold. There was a pile of presents stacked high on top and two beautiful reindeer to pull it along the snowy lane. James glanced at Mandy, stuck both hands deep in his pockets, and raised his shoulders in a contented sigh.

"All right, you two!" Emily Hope called from the drive. "We haven't got much time. I'll race you there!"

Mandy grinned. Her mom was dressed in a brown velvet hat with a fake-fur brim, a long, dark, Russian-style coat, and long boots. She looked too dressed up to race, Mandy thought. "Can't we wait for Don?" she pleaded.

"No!" came the instant reply. Don was still busy checking the harness. "Father Christmas doesn't like having folk around when he gets here. He's a wee bit on the shy side, like young James there!" He winked, and James blushed. "You go on ahead," he told them. "Go and enjoy yourselves!"

So they had to say good-bye for now to Rudolph and Dasher.

"Twenty minutes to go," Mandy's mom said as they set off on foot.

"I hope Dad gets back in time," Mandy said. As luck would have it, the phone had rung and he'd had to go out. "A vet's life," he'd sighed. "Always on call, always having to go and tend the sick and wounded!"

"Aah!" they'd cried. Mandy and James had felt truly sorry for him.

"Pay no attention," Emily Hope had told them. "He's only fishing for sympathy!"

So now they walked quickly along the lane in a three-some — Mandy, James, and Dr. Emily. As they drew near the main street, they saw a row of parked cars and heard carols playing over the loudspeakers. Then they saw the square. It basked in a glow of lights — yellow, red, and green. A giant Christmas tree stood proudly in the middle, all lit up. A huge crowd was gathered around it.

Mandy felt a thrill of excitement. There were children running around or perched on grown-ups' shoulders. There was Walter leaning on his garden gate, watching events, the Parker Smythes standing with Sam Western. Simon was talking to Jean, and shy Brandon Gill and his father stood munching on mince pies.

Then Julian Hardy came out of the pub to conduct the singing. He handed out carol sheets. Everyone stood ready.

"There are hundreds of people here!" James tried to count but gave up.

Mandy smiled at her mom, then slid in among the crowd. She took a song sheet, on the lookout for her father, but instead she spied Grandma and Grandpa. They gave her a wave. She waved back, continuing to thread her way toward the front.

"While shepherds watched their flocks by night,
All seated on the ground,
The angel of the Lord came down,
And glory shone around!"

Faces in the crowded square were lit by lantern light. They opened their mouths and sang. The music floated into the night sky, a chorus of happy voices.

> *"Away in a-a man-ger,*
> *No-o crib for a bed . . ."*

Mandy sang her heart out. But where was her dad? Surely he should have finished his call by now. She edged sideways out of the crowd, to look down the road for the Animal Ark Land Rover.

But there, by the side of the Fox and Goose, she was waylaid by the strange sight of two Father Christmases arguing.

"Aye, well, when I heard they were short of someone to do the job, I thought I'd better step in." A grumpy voice growled from behind a fake white beard. The figure was hidden behind a red hood and cloak, but Ernie's trousers and sturdy boots were unmistakable.

"Yes, and that was very kind of you!"

Mandy opened her eyes wide. Here, too, was a voice she recognized.

"It was really very thoughtful, Mr. Bell. But now I think you should leave it all to me!"

This figure was short and round, with a big chest beneath the red, fur-trimmed coat. The hood was pulled way up, and the voice was muffled behind an outsized white beard. But it was true; Mrs. Ponsonby was taking charge as usual. "I know how to deal with small children, you see. You might frighten the poor little things. Now step aside and let me pass. We mustn't disappoint our public, must we?"

Ernie muttered and grumbled. He wasn't going to give in without a fight. "Look here, I had to borrow this lot from the wardrobe department at the Welford Players. They didn't let me have it for nothing, neither!"

Mrs. Ponsonby eyed the moth-eaten costume as if to say that Ernie had been robbed. She smoothed her own posh costume and stroked her beard. Mandy choked back a laugh.

"Break it up there!" Julian Hardy stepped in with a smile between the two would-be Father Christmases. The carols soared on. No one except Mandy had seen or heard the squabble. "Didn't you hear? The real Father Christmas got back safely after all!"

"Surely not?"

"Well, I never!" Mrs. Ponsonby and Ernie were stunned into silence. They unhooked their beards and threw back their hoods in the shadow of the pub wall. Suddenly the music changed. Bells jingled through the loudspeakers. All the children squeezed to the very front and peered up the street.

A roar of voices struck up with the first lines of Rudolph's song as Father Christmas's sleigh came into sight.

It was magical. Rudolph and Dasher pranced toward the square. The sleigh was all lit up with tiny white lights, and silver bells jangled; it shone and sparkled as the reindeer drew near.

"Father Christmas!" the small ones gasped.

"Is he real?"

"Oh, look, it's Rudolph!"

They all looked on in wonder.

Father Christmas sat up high, holding the reins — a round man with a red face and a big white beard. He was definitely the most believable Father Christmas Mandy had ever seen.

Mandy felt James creep up alongside her. "Doesn't Don look great?" she said.

"Shh!" He glanced around to make sure that no one heard. "Don't spoil it!"

They grinned at each other. Don McNab certainly looked realistic as he stopped the sleigh in the square and stepped down. His loud voice boomed out a great "Ho-ho-ho!"

"What do you think of him?" a voice asked quietly over their shoulders. "The gentleman got here on time, just like I promised." The voice had a definite Scottish accent.

"Don!" Mandy and James jumped sky-high.

"But you're . . ."

"You should be up . . ."

They stopped dead. Don grinned back. He stood there large as life in his thick sweater and jacket. "Och, no," he protested. "You didn't still think *I* was the old man! Do you not believe in the real Father Christmas, after all I've told you?"

They gulped.

"They do now." Emily Hope smiled as she passed by with a collection box. She shook it in time to the tune. People reached deep in their pockets and gave generously. They said it was the best Christmas sleigh they'd ever seen.

When Mandy and James turned again to quiz Don, the Scotsman had melted away into the crowd.

Then there were gifts for the small children. They went up shyly one by one to whisper their Christmas wish. Father Christmas delved into the pile of wrapped presents and found the right one. The child went off hugging the parcel while moms and dads added money to the collection boxes. The line seemed to go on forever, as kids with shining eyes got to stroke Father Christmas's reindeer.

At last all the carols had been sung, the presents given out. Collectors returned to the pub with their tins, where Grandma and Grandpa Hope counted up the total. More mince pies were eaten, and then the crowd lined up along the street, ready for Father Christmas's sleigh to move on toward Beechtrees.

"He's due to make a special stop," Mandy's mom explained. She stood between Mandy and James, waiting to hear Grandpa's announcement of the grand total.

Grandpa climbed onto the sleigh, sheet of paper in hand. He asked for quiet. The music faded, the excited voices died. Clearing his throat, he read from the paper. "We have collected a grand total of eight hundred and seventy-nine pounds and thirty pence!" he announced proudly. "Which, I'm delighted to say, means Alex and her family will be off to the States as soon as possible in the New Year! Well done, everyone, and thank you very much!"

Grandpa got down from the sleigh to a round of applause. Then the crowd formed a long procession behind the sleigh.

"Come on." Emily Hope put her arms around Mandy and James's shoulders. "We can't miss the best part!" She led them into the procession. They walked slowly to the jingle of bells and the click of the reindeer's hooves.

Before they knew it, they were outside the bungalow, underneath the tall trees. Father Christmas drew the reindeer to a halt. "Ho-ho-ho!" he greeted the people at the house.

William appeared at the front window. He pulled back the curtain, gasped, then shot off. Soon the door opened and he stood on the porch, eyes bright, as Father Christmas beckoned him.

"Go on, William!" Mrs. Hastings appeared behind her son and whispered softly. She put a hand on his shoulder and nudged him down the step. He ran down the path, shook hands with the figure in red, and took a huge present from him. His mom stood by, smiling.

"Say thank you," she prompted.

William could hardly see over his mysterious box. "Thank you!" he whispered.

"And thank you, from Alex's dad and me, too," Mrs. Hastings told Mandy. "Your grandpa tells me we can all go to America for Alex's operation." Quickly she brushed a tear away as Jeremy Hastings hurried inside to fetch their daughter. She took Mandy in her arms and gave her a great big hug.

And now it was Alex's turn. She came to the step with her dad, all wrapped up in her coat, scarf, and hat, carrying Amber. The kitten blinked at the lights on the sleigh.

"Here, give her to me," Mr. Hastings urged Alex.

As if in a daze, she handed Amber over and came slowly down the path. Father Christmas welcomed her with open arms. She smiled up at him, a dazzling, disbelieving smile. Then he lifted her clean off her feet and into the sleigh.

"Choose a present!" he boomed.

Alex pointed shyly to a small, round parcel. All the people who had helped to make this the best Christmas ever looked on, as she tore off the wrapping. Inside was a tiny blue leather collar with a silver bell. She held it up to show Mandy. "Look! He must have got the letter. He brought this for Amber!"

Her dad came forward with a smile and handed her the kitten. Carefully, Alex fitted the collar around Amber's neck.

"Would you like a ride?" Father Christmas let her and the kitten snuggle up close.

Wide-eyed, she stared up at him and nodded. "Can William come, too?"

"Plenty of room!" Father Christmas replied.

No sooner said than done, Jeremy Hastings hoisted his son up on the sleigh.

Then Father Christmas took up the reins. "Gee up,

Rudolph! Gee up, Dasher!" The reindeer jerked once, then they were smoothly in step, clicking down the road.

Mandy and James ran to keep up. Behind them, the crowd struck up another verse from "Rudolph."

Father Christmas joined in the song as he drove his sleigh along the snowy road. His deep voice boom-boomed through the clear night air.

Mandy and James stopped dead.

"You don't think . . . ?" James stared and stammered.

Mandy swallowed hard. "No!" Father Christmas was fat and jolly, his beard was white. Her dad's was brown. "Then again, where *is* Dad right this minute?"

They watched as the sleigh turned and came back toward them.

"Magnificent, eh?"

Mandy whirled round at the sound of the familiar deep voice. "Dad!" He stood behind them, wrapped in his scarf and hat.

"What's wrong? I said I'd be back in time for the celebrations, didn't I?"

"B-but!" She gazed again at the splendid red figure on the sleigh.

Adam Hope smiled broadly and clapped his gloved hands. "Merry Christmas!" he shouted above the jingling bells.

The sleigh drew up beside them, the reindeer grunted and shook their harnesses. Alex held tight to her kitten. She and William beamed at them. Then Mr. Hastings came and lifted the children down to the ground.

Finally, the old gentleman looked Mandy and James straight in the eye. He gave one of his booming ho-ho-ho laughs. "Merry Christmas!" he said. They waved up at him, as he took the reins and drove off. "Merry Christmas, everyone!"